I0642027

Albany De Fonblanque

**Bad luck**

Vol. II: A novel

Albany De Fonblanque

**Bad luck**
*Vol. II: A novel*

ISBN/EAN: 9783743418660

Manufactured in Europe, USA, Canada, Australia, Japa

Cover: Foto ©Andreas Hilbeck / pixelio.de

Manufactured and distributed by brebook publishing software (www.brebook.com)

Albany De Fonblanque

**Bad luck**

# A Novel.

BY

## ALBANY DE FONBLANQUE,

AUTHOR OF "A TANGLED SKEIN," "CUT ADRIFT,"
ETC., ETC.

IN THREE VOLUMES.
VOL. II.

LONDON:

## RICHARD BENTLEY AND SON.

1877.

(*All Rights Reserved.*)

# CONTENTS OF VOL. II.

# BAD LUCK.

## CHAPTER I.

"MEN MAY COME AND MEN MAY GO,
BUT I GO ON FOR EVER."

N three days if all go well, the church bells of Beckhampton will ring a wedding peal. The bridegroom to be spends his birthday at the latter place going into accounts, signing releases, and finding out how much, or rather little, of his cake is left. He arrives there just in time to see the last of the auction at the mill houses, and to take leave of old Hazeltine. As the oldest tenant on the estate he ought to have taken the chair at the festivities to be held at the Hall to celebrate the young squire's wedding, but his passage is engaged and the *Black Ball* clipper that is to carry him and his wife to the other side of the world, knows naught of marryings or givings in marriage, and will not wait a day.

"We should be poor hands at merrymaking, Master Fraser," he says, "and I'm glad for one thing we shan't be here. It's a sharp wrench now it's come, and the sooner we're off the better it will be for us; but we'll drink your health and the young lady's heartily, all the same. Be sure of that."

"I thank you, Hazeltine; and will wish

you a good voyage, and all prosperity in your new home," says Fraser. " I hope the things sold well."

" Well enough. They'd have gone better if there had been anybody after the mill, but there isn't. I'm mightily afraid, Master Fraser, you won't let it in a hurry. Why look at the Beck to-day ! There isn't water enough to shake a bull-rush, let alone turn a pair of stones. And if this hot weather brings on heavy rain—as it will do or I'm mistaken—there'll be a flood come rattling down the valley, fit to tear the place down ! It's always too little, or too much now ; all along of them draining fid-fads."

" Yes, but those fid-fads, as you call them, have nearly doubled the value of the Framlington meadows—well, Pryor says so, and he knows. Why do you shake

18—2

your head, you old unbeliever? Do you
think streams are only made to grind corn?
We've got to grow it, Hazeltine, and make
them help us."

"I don't believe in making God
A'mighty's rivers into drains," growls the
miller. "You wait till them new dyeing
works is started, and see if you catch
another trout."

"I'll pitch into any one who poisons the
water, and I won't let it poison the land.
Fair play all round. Oh! by-the-bye,
talking of trout reminds me, what about
Kate? Has she changed her mind?"

"No, sir, she stays behind."

"And takes care of the mill?"

"She'll keep her own room in the house
for the present."

"Exactly. Now just tell her, please, or
get your wife, that would be better—that

I have spoken to Miss Marston about her (Kate I mean), and that she will gladly have her as maid when we come back. Or if she likes, she can go to the Hall as soon as you all leave, and live with Mrs. Aymes. I wanted Miss Marston to take her at once, but she doesn't like the idea of travelling with a maid, and to tell you the truth we haven't too much room in the yacht. But it shan't make any difference to Kate. Mrs. Aymes will engage her, and her wages will begin to-morrow if she likes."

Old Hazeltine shook his head.

" No, sir, she's too proud for that. She'd never take a shilling she did not earn. I know her."

" Well, let her go to the Hall and wait. Surely that is better for a young girl than living alone."

"It's mighty kind of you, sir—mighty kind," says the miller. "She ought to jump at it; but she's a queer girl, is Kate, I don't rightly understand her."

Fraser recalled that conversation with Mrs. Hazeltine and meanly proceeded to pump her lord.

"Do you think she has a fancy for any one about here?"

"Lord, no! To hear her scoff and sneer at the young chaps is a caution. They're all afraid of her. No, no, it ain't that. If you'll believe it, sir, she's a teaching herself French! She ain't going to let herself go cheap, I can tell you."

"I'm glad she is learning French," Fraser replies, "we shall go abroad almost every year for a few months, and it will be very useful to her."

He had quite made up his mind, you

see, that Kate was to enter his household. It was one of his peculiarities to believe that every one wanted to do what he wanted to be done for them; and as his intentions were mostly kind and generous, he was not often disappointed. You could not say that he was bumptious, or even patronizing, but still there was something that jarred. There was too much of the " I, by myself, I " about him; even Madge felt it, and this was perhaps what made her wish she had refused him—once. He had not left her a wish ungratified; he was tender and loving in a manly way. She got all she wanted, except the feeling that it was gotten by herself as an entity, and not as a part of himself. In something of the same way he took possession of Kate Vane's future. It was right that she should be provided for—he wanted to provide for her—what else could there possibly be to consider, or to do ?

The above conversation is held on the mill dam, whither old Hazeltine has retired to get out of the way and smoke his pipe in peace.  He has been cheery enough about going away, hitherto ; but each tap of the auctioneer's hammer seems as though it were driving a nail in his coffin.  He cannot hold on to the " things " to the very last, as his wife does, and praise them, and tell their history, and bid the auctioneer not to be so fast like a good man.  Women like to croon over their troubles, I have observed, and men to put them out of sight, or—pelican-like—to hide their heads and fancy they do not see them.  The mill yard is full of tax-carts and waggons in which the neighbours have brought their wives and daughters, and

intend to carry away their purchases. It
seems to the miller as though a funeral
were going on, and that these are the
hearses to bear off the dead ; and this idea
is strengthened by the presence of sundry
old ladies who only come out to funerals
and auctions and who sit round his wife
with their handkerchiefs in their laps and
exchange whispers about crockery and
glass, as though these were the dear
departed.

The last lot is disposed of, and now
there arise sounds of eating and drinking
from the dismantled house. You cannot
expect people to come twenty or thirty
miles for the chance of picking up a
bargain if you don't feed them. The
auctioneer is in the chair, and the roast
and the boiled are going, going ! at a fine
rate. Many of the convives are eating

with what are now their own knives and forks, off their plates and dishes, and drinking out of their proper glasses. These are a little exercised—the female detachment especially—over the rather rough and tumble service. It becomes a joke to call out such warnings as "Holloa, Jim, mind what you're a doing with them plates! they cost me nine shillings a dozen;" or "There now! there goes one of my half-crown decanters." Explanations as to "Why I didn't go that other sixpence, and let you have them sheets;" are current; and revenge is taken upon such as chuckle over bargains, "Why Lord bless you! I mind when it" (the bargain) "was up at old John Giane's sale, I do. That were six years ago, and it only fetched five guineas then." Every one knows every one else's ways and means, and some surprise is expressed at Jane Brumley's buying the parlour set. " Brumley can't afford it," is the general verdict. But the parlour set is sold, and the auctioneer has the money; so let us hope that Brumley is in a better way than his kind neighbours suppose.

Then the packing up and the carrying away begin. There is lamentation about heretofore undiscovered cracks, and mendings ; and over some modern breakages which take the gilt off the gingerbread. There are borrowings of " a bit of rope for my old woman's clothes press," and " room in your cart, as you ain't brought nothing, for that there cask of cider ;" and so on ; which amuse Fraser Ellicott, and even call up a grim smile on his companion's pale face.

Fraser is invited to the feast, but does

not go in.  His benevolent intentions for
Kate are confided to her uncle this time,
because poor Mrs. Hazeltine is quite
broken down by the worry of preparing
for the sale, and the excitement of behold-
ing her long loved "things" knocked
down, and scattered over the country.
She clings to them still, though they are
irrevocably "gone," and has something to
say over each lot as it is carried out.
When it is about time for him to go,
Fraser finds her watching with many a
sigh and turn of the head, the departure in
a tax cart of six high-backed old fashioned
mahogany chairs ; manufactured in some
dark age for the development of spinal
diseases.

"You're a lucky woman, Jane Brumley,"
she informs the fortunate purchaser, " to
have such a set of cheers as them, and you

not married a year ! Use them well, Jane, and they'll be a credit to your grand-children. But don't ye, now, go putting any o' that sticky stuff I see you daubing over your furniture t'other day, on *them.* It looks slick enough at first, Jane, but it ain't no use ; spoils the cheers and the coats of them as sits in 'em, and draws the dust like a tea leaf. No, Jane Brumley, I've had 'em thirty year come Christmas, and I ought to know what's good for 'em. Elbow grease twice a week, and some bees' wax and turpentine—very little 'turps, Jane—once a month. Do ye, like a good girl, take care of them cheers, Jane."

" Why of course I shall," says Jane rather tartly. She does not like to have her French polish called " sticky stuff." " I suppose they're mine now," and off she drives with them, leaving the bereaved proprietor of their middle age, sobbing with her apron thrown over her head.

" Now look here, Mrs. Hazeltine," says Fraser, " this won't do at all. You'll fret yourself quite ill this way. What the deuce does it matter what they do with a lot of old furniture, so that they pay for it ?"

" They were bits of home, Master Fraser," she answers, with tears in her eyes ; " just as your bones are bits of you. It almost breaks my heart to see them go."

" Then don't see them go. Shut your eyes and harden your heart, and go up-stairs and have a cup of tea. Hazeltine's got something to say to you, and I want it all settled before you leave. When do you go ?"

" To-morrow by the 6.50 train to Liver-pool. We're all packed up and ready, thank God ! and I wish it were to-morrow now. Oh look ye there—do ! If that stupid old Clayton ain't taking off the chaney set Aunt Martha left me, in a washing tub without a bit of straw or nothing, and his cart——"

" There, never mind old Clayton," says Fraser stopping her; " go up and get your tea. I'll wish you good-bye in the morning."

He is as good as his word, though it rains heavily. There is a great crowd of neighbours and friends assembled at the station to wish the Hazeltines good-bye, and throw old shoes after them. He sees them off without another word about Kate. That of course has been settled. Just before they leave the up-train comes in, and Mr. Henry Wybert steps out of it on the opposite platform.

"Just the very thing," says Fraser Ellicott to himself as he breaks the law, and runs across.

"Look here, Wybert," he shouts; "the Hazeltines are going away to Australia, now. The train will start in two minutes, won't you come and wish them good-bye?"

"Do you presume, sir, after—" Wybert begins loftily.

"Oh, bah! let all that go. Come and wish them good-bye, and shake hands over it. To day's my birthday. I'll apologise and—and all that, if you like. I want to be friends with everybody to-day. Come."

Wybert allows himself to be half led, half dragged across, just as the other train snorts its "I'm off!"

"Here they are," shouts Fraser struggling through the crowd, and making for the window out of which old Hazeltine's head is thrust in the act of giving a last kiss to weeping Kate Vane. " Hold on a minute—here's Wybert !"

But trains don't hold on for partings. This one pants on out of the station, a woman screams, and Fraser sees Kate make three steps and a totter; and then fall as though she were shot through the heart. Fortunately Mr. Wybert is there to catch her.

" Poor girl !" says Fraser when she recovers ; " she was fond of them after all. Here, Waters !" (this to the usual flyman, who was in attendance), " take Miss Vane up to the old Hall, and tell Mrs. Aymes to send for her things as she may direct." He has not a notion that she has scornfully rejected his offer, and she has not breath to tell him so. Away she is driven to the old Hall, and its master takes Mr.

Wybert by the elbow and leads him out of the station. " This is my birthday," he repeats; " and I want to make friends. I'm going to give a dinner at the Rose and Crown. Duty sort of business, you know —won't be very gay. There's the Rector, and old May of the bank, and Pryor and his son, and Lord ! I forgot my guardian, Mr. Temple Fluery—ever such a swell ! just your sort — and — and one or two more. Now I do want you to come, smoke the calumet of peace, and bury the hatchet."

" I have not come here to go to dinners, Mr. Ellicott," he replies haughtily, shaking free his arm.

" What for then ? To fast ?"

" I am here to wish my mother fare-well."

" What ! are you really off, then ?"

" I cannot imagine how my movements can interest you, sir; but if my answer will shorten this, to me, unpleasant conversation, I will reply, ' I sail for the West Indies to-morrow.' "

" That's no reason why you shouldn't dine with me to-day."

" I decline your invitation."

" Well, shake hands at any rate."

" I will not take the hand of a man who has raised it against me."

" Now, Wybert, don't be an ass! If you had been placed as I was, you'd have done as I did, and serve me ri— No, I won't say that. I'll stick to what I said just now. I'll apologise. I was too rough, and I dare say you'd have done the right thing if I had gone to work in a more—well, hang it! in a more gentlemanly way. There, now!"

"I will not accept such an apology, and I'll stick to what *I* said. I will not forgive, and I will not forget," said Wybert deliberately.

"Then it is war to the knife."

"It is war."

"Well, as you are going to Barbadoes, and I'm staying here, we shall have to fire rather long shots."

"Long shots are heavy ones."

"When they hit."

"They will hit."

"Then, damn it all!" cries Fraser, losing his temper, "look out for yourself; for if I get a chance I'll smash you."

As he spoke, Mrs. Wybert turned the corner, hurrying, no doubt, to meet her son at the station in spite of the weather. He joined her, and when they had walked on some eight or ten steps, she turned and gave Fraser Ellicott a look which he had good cause to remember.

" A pair of them," he muttered ; " but I was a fool to fly out like that."

Ay ! that he was.

The dinner was not the dull affair its Amphytrion prophesied. On the contrary it was hearty and pleasant, from the soup to the cigars. Even the speeches—of course there were speeches—did not bore any one. No cold shoulder now. The Rector, who proposed Fraser's health, spoke very nicely of Madge, and without hinting that there had ever been anything whispered against her, said for her what delicately covered the ground. The elder guests departed about ten o'clock, and left the rest to enjoy their weeds, and talk over the new cricket club that was to be formed, and the piscicultural works promised by the young squire, which were to fill the Beck with trout in defiance of all the bleaching works could do.

"I'll walk down with you as far as the bridge," he said to Sam Pryor when they broke up. "It's awfully hot after the rain."

"There'll be more before morning," Sam prophesied.

"Yes. Old Hazeltine said there would be. How he went on about the drought and the floods! Are the floods bad?"

"Oh no. They rise quickly, but they don't last long," said Sam.

They parted on the bridge, and whether Fraser had got better by Madge's "thinking " mania, or the still night disposed him to thought, need not be considered. He lit another cigar, and leaned over the parapet. Under his eyes dashed the swollen Beck; on his right slumbered the town. On the other side loomed the high wall belonging to the "fives" court of Dr. Byng's school. At its foot, hid in shadow, ran the path through the meadows along the margin of the stream, where he had walked that Sunday and been called "sir." All was still as the grave ; as ever, when a tempest is brewing. On the parapet, close to where he stood, was a large stone, round and smooth almost like a cricket ball. Some small boys had been playing "conqueror" with its likes, and this one, perhaps, had won the day. Fraser took it up and tossed it idly from hand to hand. Of a sudden he heard footsteps. The figure of a man passed quickly along the path, and mounted the steps which led to the bridge. There came a low growl of thunder, and heavy drops began to fall.

# CHAPTER II.

### THE RISING OF THE WATERS.

E must now go back and see what passed between mother and son, as Mr. Wybert and the widow walked home in the rain.

" How came you to speak to that man again ?" she asked him angrily.

" He forced himself upon me. Wanted to make friends, and asked me to his birth-day party." Every word a sneer.

" Of course you declined the honour."

"Of course. Did you hear what he said?"

"'If I get a chance I'll smash you.' He's a low brute. I'd have the law of him, Henry, if I were you."

"Pshaw!" he scoffed. "Bluster—nothing more. I'll be even with him some day, without any law. Leave him to me. Why did not you tell me that the Hazeltines were going away?"

"It was no business of mine or yours. They've gone, and joy go with them. A pretty scandal they leave behind! and they to call themselves decent people! It's disgusting. Is my lady that is to be, as pretty as my lady's-maid that is to be?"

"I really don't understand you, mother."

"Listen. That man who is going to be married this week—who asks all the place to hobnob with him, and wish him joy—

this precious Mr. Fraser Ellicott we are all to bow down and worship—when he was here last month, haunted the Mill after that girl on the pretence of fishing. He had the impertinence to come to my house with his rubbishing trout, and try to throw dust in my eyes. He wasn't after fish at the Mill, Henry; he was after a human soul with his snares and his devices, and the devil helped him to catch it. That hussy, Kate Vane, remains behind and is engaged as lady's-maid at the Hall. What do you think of that?"

Mr. Wybert bit his lip, and kept his thoughts to himself. He remembered now what Fraser had said to the flyman.

"You are not fair upon the girl," he replied after a pause, " or on him either. He is not as bad as that; a year or two hence, perhaps, he will come to such a thing—not now.  He is marrying for what he calls love."

" Brutes such as he is don't know what love is.  Not one man in ten does.  Not one in a thousand would resist a girl as pretty as Kate Vane, who threw herself at his head.  We'll see."

By this time they had arrived at the cottage, where breakfast awaited them. The day was cold and dark and dreary. The rain poured down steadily till about five o'clock, when there was a lull.  Mr. Wybert rose and put on his hat and coat.

"Henry !" said his mother reproachfully, " are you going out ?  There is little time left for us to pass together, and you may not find me when you return."

" I am not sure about the train," he replied, " and—and have some orders to give about my baggage. I will not be long, dear mother ; I wish to spend my last minutes with you, and it is better to be sure."

He was quite sure about his train, and had no baggage at the station. That had gone on before him. There was one train at half-past nine and another about midnight, either of which would take him to Southampton in time for the mail steamer. He did not go to the station, but to the hotel to which the fly which had taken Kate Vane to the old Hall, belonged ; and found the driver smoking his pipe in the taproom, alone.

" I had something rather important to say to my old friends the Hazeltines," Mr. Wybert began, " but had no time in the confusion—my train was late, you know—and as I don't know exactly where to write to them, I want to see Miss Vane for a minute or two, and ask."

" Well, sir, she's at the Hall," said the flyman.

" To tell you the truth, Waters; Mr. Ellicott and I are not quite good friends (no fault of mine), and I don't like to go to his house. Couldn't you go up and ask her to step into the road just for five—or stop" (taking out his pocket-book and writing on a page which he tore out and gave to the man), "hand her this ; there'll be half a sovereign for you, Waters, when you come back."

Waters earned the money.

*        *        *        *

Kate Vane, scarce recovered from her first fainting fit when she was huddled into the fly, went off into another, and knew not what was happening to her till she found herself on a sofa very wet about the hair and neck ; and Mrs. Aymes leaning over her with smelling-salts.

" There, there ! Don't ye cry, my dear ; lie still like a good girl," said the house-keeper, " and you'll be all right by dinner time."

" Where am I ?" asked Kate dreamily.

" Where you're going to be happy, I hope, my dear, and well taken care of ; you're a lucky girl, Kate. There ain't many as has your chance. Mr. Fraser says you're to send for your things when you like, and you needn't do nothing till the young lady comes."

" He sent me here then ? you are Mrs. Aymes ?" said Kate, rising upon one elbow and thrusting the dank hair from her brow. " He sent me here when—let me get up, Mrs. Aymes. I will—"

The will was all there, but not the strength to carry it out. She fell back with a groan.

"It was cowardly," she moaned. "Oh, how I hate him!"

"Hate Mr. Fraser!" cried the old lady aghast. The idea of any one hating her nursling and master!

"Yes," the girl repeated through clenched teeth, "hate him, do you hear? Hate him, hate him, hate him! is that clear enough?"

"You must be crazy!"

"I shall be if I stay here much longer. What right had he to send me to his house?"

"Why, I thought it was all settled that you was to come for his wife's maid!"

"Settled! Look here, Mrs. Aymes. He came to the Mill with his insolent,

overbearing, patronising airs. Chaffs me
—that would be his word !—*chaffs* me about
marrying your clod-hoppers : would he
dare have said about a girl in his own
world what he said about me ; and before
my face ? Then he goes behind my back
to aunt and uncle, tries to break up all my
plans, tries to make mischief between us
when we had settled—yes, *settled* everything our own way. Who was he that he
should interfere ? I told them I would
rather beg my bread from door to door
than owe it to him, and I would have told
him the same if he had given me an
opportunity. I never accepted his service ;
but because my grand young lord so wills
it, he supposes I am to go down on my
knees and take what he flings me. I'll die
first ! To crown all, he takes advantage
of my having fainted at the station, and

sends me like a box or a dog to his house.
Pah ! the air of it sickens me."

" You'll be better by-and-by, my dear,"
said Mrs. Aymes dryly. " You don't know
what you are talking about."

" I hope I shall be better by-and-by,
and then I shall know what I will *do*,
madam."

" I never heard such awful ingratitude,"
cried the housekeeper, raising her hands ;
" never ! and if I was to stop and hear
any more I should give you a bit of my
mind you wouldn't like. I've no patience
with such a girl—well, well ! you're upset
at losing your people and that. Try and
sleep a bit. It'll do you good. Don't
mind me. I love Mr. Fraser as though
he were my own son, and it looks like
flying in the face of Providence—there !
don't go talking back on me. Go or stay,

I don't allow that, Kate Vane. I'll darken the room, and fetch you a cup of tea by-and-by. Say your prayers, and ask God to put these wicked thoughts out of your heart, and make a good girl of you."

Kate buried her face in the pillow, and sobbed till weariness and the darkened room had their effect. When good Mrs. Aymes came, by-and-by, with the cup of tea, she found her sleeping—the first sleep she had had for many nights and days. It was past six o'clock when she woke; she was alone, refreshed, desperate. A dim idea that she was caught and caged— terrible from its very dimness—began to grow in her overwrought mind. She must escape, and now was the time. Her hat and waterproof were there. The house was silent. If she could only slip down-

stairs, and out.   No one in the lobby, no
one in the hall, and the door unlocked.
Victory! she was free.   As she ran down
the drive she heard footsteps and hid.   A
man had just passed the lodge-gates—the
driver of the fly.   What luck!   He could
take her home.

"Lord, how you scared me, miss!" he
exclaimed, as she darted out on him from
the hedge of evergreens.

"Get your carriage at once, Mr.
Waters," she gasped, "and take me home,
for God's sake."

"Willingly, miss, but first of all read
this," and he gave her Mr. Wybert's note.

Ten minutes afterwards she flung herself
upon a man who was waiting in the road
—not into his arms, for they did not open
to receive her, but upon him, as on one
who ought to have folded her to his

bosom. Their words were quick, short and earnest. When they parted she turned up her face to him and he kissed her on the forehead.

" I did not think it had gone so far," he mused as he walked back towards Mrs. Wybert's cottage. " Lucky she does not know I am going away, or there would be a scene. How she hates that Ellicott ! And my good mother—well, let it be so. I've half a mind to make her stay there. She would do so—for me ; and to have a girl like that, who hates him, under his roof, might not be amiss ; but then I'd have to tell her about Barbadoes, and she'd want to come. That would never do. What a world it is ! I've won this woman body and soul, I believe, if I wanted either, in just the same way that lost me Madge Marston."

And this was in some degree true. He had schooled and snubbed Miss Vane, as indeed he did most people beneath him in years or station, but her wild wayward heart—she could not tell herself when or how—warmed to him, and then his coldest words had a charm, and every reproof was glorified into an evidence of affection.

*He was making a lady of her,* poor little fool! She was going to marry a gentleman as her mother did, but unlike her mother she would not shame him. This was her dream night and day; for this she tried to educate herself; for this she refused to accompany her relatives to Australia, and out of it came her hatred to well-meaning Fraser Ellicott. She marry a bumpkin! She take service! Small provocation was there, truly, for such anger as she felt, but enough to stir her passionate nature into a storm.

" I shall have to go by the half-past nine train, I find," said Mr. Wybert on his return. " It is a great disappointment, dear mother; for I did so hope I could stay with you till nearly midnight."

" And you will be away three whole years?" she said, half to herself.

" Perhaps not so long ; perhaps——"

" Well ?"

" Strange things will happen sometimes. I am not off yet."

" You are hankering after that girl, Henry."

" What girl ?" he began with a start, but checked himself. "Oh, you mean Miss Marston."

"Who else should I mean? It is a good thing for you that you were saved from your own folly. You might look higher than to her, my son. Still I hate the idea of your being supplanted by that cub Ellicott. You did like the girl, and I believe it is all through her that you are going away. I detest the minx, and I don't care who sees and knows it."

"Let us talk of something else, mother, please."

"You are a tame creature, Henry. Take after your father. If you had more of my blood in your veins, you'd never sit down under the insults he has heaped upon you. Why you sneaked off like a whipped cub after the threat he made this morning!"

"Leave him to me," he replied gloomily; "I will be even with Mr. Ellicott in my own way, and in my own time. He may claim a victory over me now, but it won't last long. I say again, strange things happen sometimes. He is not married yet, and I—I am not at Barbadoes."

"Tell me what is in your mind. Trust your mother, Henry; I am not a demonstrative woman—never was, but I do love you, my son, and this separation makes me very sad."

"There is nothing in my mind which takes a definite shape," he replied; "only a feeling that—I cannot describe it. It is here; I can say no more; and so strong it is, that I have not yet taken my passage in the steamer. If I go, I must trust to chance for a berth; but there is sure to be room. Now tell me more about Ellicott and that girl, Kate Vane. Was it before

or after he came here last that she refused
to go with the Hazeltines?"

" How should I know?"

" I think it will turn out that it was before; and if this be so, he cannot have had
anything to do with it; because he had not
been here for two years. You must not be
so hard upon Kate Vane, mother."

" Oh, you're taking her part now—are
you? She is fortunate to have so many
gentlemen to look after her. Perhaps you
and Mr. Ellicott are rivals again for this
hussy?"

" I think, mother," he said, flushing up,
and biting his lip, " that considering the
little time which we have left together, you
might spare me such very random taunts."

" You began the subject."

" I asked you to tell me what you knew
about this girl and Ellicott. You appear

to know nothing, and therefore have no right to make such insinuations."

"I know what I know. What business had he down here just at the time when he was first engaged to Miss Marston? Fishing! Do men like that leave London in June for such fishing as there is in the Beck? And he engages her, an untried girl, who has never been in service before, to be my fine lady's own maid! What does she know of lady's-maiding, and what does that pauper parson's daughter want with a maid? Gentlemen did not engage their wives' female servants when I was a girl."

\*     \*     \*     \*     \*

"It might do, by God! it might do," muttered Mr. Wybert when he had parted with his mother and was out again in the dark stormy night; "if I could only get her to work it without knowing why. She hates him enough to do him any mischief, and she loves me. I wonder if she knows about his marriage ? If I let her think I wanted to break it off, she'd suspect. No, that's not the way. Tell her he has been bragging about her stopping behind for him—to be near him ; yes, that's better. Get her to write a remonstrance which will read two ways ; manage for it to fall into Madge's hands. That would stop the marriage—even that would be something. Let me see, I could be at Laremouth to-morrow, and yet have— By Heaven ! I'll try."

The half-past nine o'clock train did not carry Mr. Wybert. He never had intended that it should. As it snorted out of the station, he was walking in one of the back slums of Beckhampton with a woman closely wrapped up in a dark waterproof cloak. It is the sort of night that one would not turn one's enemy's dog out into; yet these two walk on slowly, away from shelter.

# CHAPTER III.

### DEW IS GOOD FOR PEARLS.

N two days, if all go well, Laremouth church bells will ring a wedding peal. There also they have kept Fraser's birthday, and preparations are going on for the greater day which is to quickly follow it. Lots of pretty presents arrive for Madge. Uncle Joe does not forget her. Her other uncle on the father's side, the earl who lives in Paris and would not leave France for a

dukedom, send her such a string of pearls !
Even the Right Honourable Temple Fluery
writes a despatch and has the honour to
inclose a morocco box containing a locket
which makes her eyes glitter as bright as
its sapphires. Bell De Gray and her boys
are at the Vicarage, and her sixpenceless
man is coming with something in his pocket
too, which will outglitter all the rest. I
don't know what they would have done
without Bell. She takes charge of everything, from the jellies to the wedding
favours. She has quickly put all the
arrangements in shape, and is now busy
packing up and correcting French milliners'
ideas of what are useful yachting costumes.
If the worst had come to the worst with
Bell, she would have made her mark as a
dressmaker ; and oh ! the ideas of Madame
Estelle who undertakes the trousseau, upon

yachting costumes ! As a yachts-woman of *Opéra Bouffe* the future Mrs. Ellicott would have been charming—*ravissante !* but not a gown had she to her back which could be worn with the least comfort in a real boat, or which a handful of spray would not have ruined.

Bell's nimble fingers went to work—not too soon—and linen and blue serge are taking useful and not unornamental shapes. Madge, I am sorry to say, is idle.

Returned to her old home, her old dreamy ways come over her again. She takes no part in the packing-up; she thinks Bell the dearest and cleverest of old things, but is of no sort of assistance to her. She haunts her thinking-place on the cliff, and cannot be got to take an interest in the proceedings in which she is to play the leading part. No one minds her. Young girls going to be wives in three days have more to think about than dresses and breakfast-cakes, and so they leave her to herself.

It is night—a hot, damp, oppressive June night, which not a breath of air has freshened. The French windows opening to the lawn are wide apart; so is the hall-door. Hard-working Bell pauses in her stitching, passes her handkerchief over brow and throat, and gasps repeatedly. Madge sits with her hands on her lap watching her. The Vicar has retired to his study, where, in a linen dressing-gown, he smokes the smoke of the blessed, and thinks of the settlements he has approved on paper, and is soon to grasp in sheepskin. No happier man than the Vicar.

"I wish you'd put down your work, Bell, dear, and talk to me," says Madge.

" I can work and talk too."

" But it fidgets me to watch your fingers."

" Don't watch them, then."

" Oh, it would be the same thing !—the click-click of your needle is so irritating. Don't work any more, darling, to-night. I'm not worth so much trouble. What does it matter ?"

" You'll find out when you get to the Mediterranean," laughs Bell. " Bless the child ! do you think that all this tom-fooling of Estelle's can be put right in a day ? Make believe that the click-click says *comfort, comfort,* Madge, and thank Heaven you've a clever old sister to fidget you."

" I do thank Heaven for that. Ah ! Bell, if I were only married four years, and safe like you."

"But, my precious, people can't be married four years all at once, can they? You are like the old lady who wouldn't let her boys bathe until they had learned to swim. You've got to begin at the beginning. Many women who have been married four years would give their eyes to go back to where you stand."

"And perhaps I may too, Bell. I would give more than my eyes to know what I shall feel this day four years."

"I'm ashamed of you! You are as bad as you were that day at my house, when you talked such utter nonsense."

"When you were so painfully wise. Don't begin again, please. I know I'm talking nonsense, but I can't help it."

"I wish I had Aladdin's carpet: I'd carry you off to Beckhampton again.

LIBRARY
UNIVERSITY OF ILLINOIS

That takes the nonsense out of you," says Bell.

"Oh! you think I value that? I want my husband's wealth to be jingled in my face like a baby's rattle, to be happy; do I?"

"No, dear," Bell replies, unheedful of her pettishness; "you want something to dispel a cloud of morbid fancies — no matter what. Dear, dear, how oppressive it is!"

"I'm a hateful thing, any way," cries Madge.

"It is fortunate that some one is not of your opinion. Take care that he never is."

"Bell, do you think that men feel disappointment like us!"

"What sort of disappointment?"

"Well, disappointment in love."

" Not *as* we do, I fancy, but quite as bitterly ; perhaps more so."

" Oh, they get over it in time."

" So do we ; only it makes them reckless and bad, whereas we only get disagreeable."

" Bell !"

" We do. Blighted young damsels who grieve in silence and white muslin with blue bows, belong to the circulating library and the French drama. In real life they only get disagreeable, and worry papa into consent. I worried papa into consent, I did ! Girls don't get into a decline when they are crossed in love, nowadays ; they get into a bad temper, and it does quite as well."

" I was not talking of girls. I asked you if men felt it so much."

" Bad temper ?"

" You know what I mean, Bell."

" I will answer you," Bell replies, putting down her work. " I once knew a man—a good man, Madge, in every sense of the word, who was driven headlong to destruction in this world and the next, because a coquette jilted him."

" Vanity."

" No, it wasn't vanity. It made him lose all faith in woman. It's an awful thing for a man, and worse perhaps for some of us, when a man loses faith in his mother's sex."

" Why, what a solemn Bell !"

" Poor fellow ! it was a hard case. The very good in him was his ruin ; but others —pshaw ! ' If she be not kind to me, what care I to whom she be !' is the burden of their song."

" Then, as a rule, you don't think they mind much ?" asked Madge.

" A good many, as you say, ' get over it.'
Are you thinking of the hearts you slaugh-
tered in town ?   I don't think you did much
damage," Bell continues gaily, resuming her
sewing.   " Remember you were ticketed
' sold,' like a picture at the Exhibition."

" 'Sold,' " Madge repeated to herself.

" Now, you must really leave off talking,
and try this on," says Bell, rising with the
blue serge.   " I just want to get the length
right—that's all.   Are not my little loops
of black braid *chic* ?"

There was not much exertion to be gone
through, but at the end Madge almost fell
back into her chair.

" Oh, by-the-bye," says Bell, when the
length had been found all right, " have
you given orders about papa's breakfast ?"

" He did not say anything to me," replies
weary Madge.

"No; well, he's going to the Bishop's visitation or charge, or something, and I heard him order the carriage for half-past six, to catch the 7.15 train. Are you going to be down at six ?"

" Perhaps."

" If I were in your place, I should make it right with Susan. You are not famed for early rising, Madge. Fancy a bishop's charge on an empty stomach !"

The bell was within easy reach of where Madge sat. She stretched out her hand languidly, and rang it twice. Susan appeared, and instructions, tending to the fortification of the Vicar against the impending ordeal, were duly given. This done, Madge relapsed into her former attitude, and the click-click of Bell's needle went on unreproved.

At last she rose, and was silently leaving the room when Bell looked up and said :

" Going to bed ?"

" No, dear ; going out."

" At this time of night ?"

" Yes ; I often do.    This heat is insupportable ; I must have a breath of fresh air if there is any."

" Well, my darling, go.    Perhaps it will do you good ; but goodness, child ! you've got on your pearls."                          .

" I forgot to take them off, and the box is upstairs," she replies, looking down at the costly beads.    " Never mind, dew is good for pearls — have you not read *Lothair* ?"

" Yes ; but nowhere in that abstruse work will you find that it is good for the throats they hang on.    So let me throw something over your head and shoulders, for you are flushed and little would give you cold. Fancy a bride with a cold in her head. Madge, dear, it would be ruin. Take my nubia——But I insist. All the rice powder in the world cannot quench a red nose. Horror! I think I see it beaming like a star through your veil. Be a good child, now," says the matron, follow-the bride-elect into the hall, and taking that nubia from the hat-rack. "There! let me wind it round your throat. Why it looks *très coquette!* Now kiss me and run away. Don't be long. What, crying?"

"You *are* so kind, you are all so kind to me, and I don't deserve it one bit," she sobs on her sister's shoulder. "Oh, Bell, dear sister, say you will love me always? Promise you will love me, whatever may happen!"

"Silly child! Promise yourself that

nothing *can* happen to take our love away —an easy promise, you poor little trembling pet—and all will go well. There, run away, or I shall do no more work to-night."

Bell De Gray is a woman of the world. Young married women who move much in society, my dear sir, are not such simple- tons as you sometimes take them to be. Do you think they never laugh at you in their Cluny lace sleeves when you trot out your sophistries, and look your unutterable things ? They know you— *are fond.* Are you so foolish as to suppose that Benedict the married respects your secrets, and keeps the cats of his bachelor friends in the bag ? Bell De Gray is a woman of the world, and up to most of its tricks, but Madge puzzles her. There is something wrong with the girl, and she cannot make it out. Poor little Madge ! She likes her for being ill

at ease.   She has known girls who said the
irrevocable " I will " with less deliberation
than they take to pull the string of their
shower-bath ; and who put on matrimony
as they would a new dress.   She is glad
that little Madge is not one of these.   Poor
little motherless, solitary Madge !   Something sends Mrs. Bell up to the chamber,
once her own, where her boys are asleep in
their cot.   There she thinks of her own
quiet wedding, and the scarcely-veiled fore-
bodings of evil which clouded it ; of the
anxieties and triumphs which followed
chance !   She scouted the idea of chance
as applied to her Horace.   He was *sure*
to be good, *sure* to succeed, *sure* to make
her happy !  but there might be chances for
poor little Madge.   Fraser was an idle
man, and somebody findeth mischief still for
idle hands to do.   " Pshaw !" she exclaimed

at last, " I shall be getting sentimental and superstitious too, if I go on brooding like this. It's all nonsense, and I must finish that dress to-night." She goes down again and finds it is much darker. Was the lamp burning dim? She turns it up, and goes on with her work. Presently she hears the servant fastening the front door.

"Don't lock up just yet, Mason," she says; " Miss Margaret is out."

" Beg your pardon, ma'am; she's gone upstairs some time."

" Indeed! I did not hear her come in."

" She come in through master's study, ma'am."

" Very well; lock up, then. Has papa gone to bed?"

" Yes, ma'am. He went up soon after Miss Margaret come in."

" I shall sit up a little longer, Mason ; I have something to do. What is the matter with the lamp ?"

" I don't think there's nothing the matter with it, ma'am," he replies. " It's the fog as makes it dark. There's an awful fog outside—come on quite sudden."

" Why, so there is !" says Bell, looking out into the hall. " I thought this hot weather would bring something. Let me have more light, then ; I really cannot get on with this."

Another lamp is brought, doors and windows closed, curtains drawn, and all made snug. Bell goes on with her labours of love ; and when at last she retires, she knocks lightly at her sister's door, whispering :

" Pleasant dreams and rosy slumbers,

darling ! I hope the fog has spared your nose. Asleep !" she says more softly. "I am glad of that. Poor little Madge !"

Bell is not an early riser. She dresses herself and the boys leisurely, and finds the table laid for four.

" Good little Madge ! She has given papa his breakfast, and is going to join me and the brats."

(Mrs. De Gray calls her olive branches " brats ;" but it wouldn't do for you or I to follow suit.)

Then she goes out in the garden. A breeze, which sprung up in the night, has blown away the fog, save in crannies and chinks in the downs, where it still hangs sulkily. Overhead it is a bright, pleasant day. As she passes the stable, the pony-carriage comes back from the station.

" Did your master catch the train ?" she asks the groom.

" Oh yes, ma'am—all right," replies the man ; " and if you please, 'm, master told me to say he shouldn't be home till late, as perhaps he should have to go to Canterbury ; and I'm to meet the nine o'clock train."

Bell hopes to herself that there is nothing wrong about the license ; and in the meantime her brats sidle shyly up to the ponies, and pat them. She saunters back to the house, and flings a handful of gravel at Madge's window, crying :

" Come down, lazybones, and give your sister her breakfast ; she's hungry !"

" Mayn't we go and hunt her out, ma ?" petitions the elder brat. " It would be such fun !"

" No, dear; perhaps poor auntie's tired ?"

" Oh, ma! it's so late, and we want our break'us," pleads the brat.

" Then you shall have it," replies the fond mother ; and in she goes.

" I do believe the wretch " (meaning Madge) " has gone to bed again," she tells herself. " I've a great mind to let them " (meaning the brats) " loose at her."

Upon second thoughts, she resolves to let them loose upon their breakfast instead, and rings the bell for Mason. •

" Did Miss Marston give papa his breakfast ?" she asks him.

" No, ma'am."

" Oh! then, Mason, perhaps if you were to bring breakfast, she would be down before it's quite ready. The children have been up some time, and say they are hungry."

" Certainly, ma'am," says Mason, and

he departs with the air of a genius of the lamp.

But he does not come back like one. Soon a whispering and a sort of scuffle is heard in the passage, which Bell does not understand. In spite of herself, it frightens her. She opens the door suddenly, and a wave of servants surges into the back regions, leaving Susan stranded, as it were, against the wall, looking deadly pale, with her hand on her side and almost breathless.

" Oh, ma'am !" she gasps, " Miss Madge isn't in the house !"

" Well, perhaps she has gone for a walk. Why don't some of you go and find her, or ring the bell ? Bless the girl ! Why do you stand there, as though you had seen a ghost ?"

" Oh, please don't talk of ghosts !" pleads

the frightened maid. "She's not gone out for a walk; she's not been in her room all night!"

"Nonsense! Mason saw her go up to bed."

"She didn't sleep in it, then. It's just as I made it yesterday. Oh dear! oh dear!"

With a sound that is half a sob and half a cry, Bell springs up the stairs. Susan is right; the room has not been slept in. There is not a sign of Madge!

By this time the servants have congregated again, with white faces and beating hearts. Bell alone is coherent.

"Come here, Mason," she says. "You told me that Miss Margaret came in through papa's study, and went to bed before you brought me the second lamp."

"Yes, ma'am; and I could have taken my Bible oath of it, till Susan——"

"Does she ever make her own bed?"

"No, never! Miss Madge make her own bed! No, ma'am!"

"Was Mason sober last night?" asks Bell.

Mason indignantly answered for himself.

"Then how could you possibly tell me you saw my sister come in?"

"Well, ma'am, *somebody* came in, and I thought it was her. I'll take my Bible oath somebody passed the pantry-window, and went into master's study by the outside door; but the fog was that thick——"

The fog! Never did that usually disagreeable word sound so sweetly in Bell's ears.

"Why, of course!" she exclaims, with something almost like a smile. "How silly of me not to think of it before ! She got overtaken in the fog, and very prudently, very properly, Mason, did not risk returning by the cliff, and has gone—to Miss Westwood's, perhaps, to spend the night. Please go round at once, and ask. Ask also at the cottages where old Mrs. Withers used to live ; she might be there. Poor little Madge ! What a fright she must have had ! But, really, she might have come, or sent to tell us word she was safe before this," Bell adds to herself. " Why, it must be past ten o'clock !"

# CHAPTER IV.

"THE BLINDING MISTS CAME UP AND HID THE LAND,

AND NEVER, NEVER MORE CAME SHE."

MISS WESTWOOD has seen nothing of Madge since noon of the day before. The cottagers where old Mrs. Withers lived know nothing about her. She does not appear to answer for herself. Bell, now almost frantic, rushes down to the village, up to the coastguard station — everywhere — seeking her in vain.

" My God! my God !" she wails. "And I let her go out! What shall I say to Fraser ? What shall I say to papa ?"

What indeed ! She is lost. But how ? Lost on the eve of a happy marriage ! How could she be lost to them but in one way ? Was she dead ? Had she gone to her thinking-place on the cliff ?—poor over-wrought child !—got overtaken by the fog, missed her path, and—— Oh, it was too horrible! Bell could not bid them search the sands below—*would* not give up hope. Oh, if Madge were playing them a trick, and hiding, she would never forgive her—never !

The post came in at twelve o'clock, and brought a letter from Fraser—the last he would ever address to Miss Marston ; the last of all, perhaps. The sight of it made poor Bell's blood curdle in her veins.

Who would open that letter now?    Twelve
o'clock! one! two!    Oh! how gladly she
would forgive any trick, however cruel,
now, so that the cruel one came to be forgiven.    Would papa never come back!
When the long day dragged to its end,
and she heard the sound of wheels upon
the gravel, he came all too soon.    What
should she say to him?    What should she
say to Fraser?

The Vicar alighted, looking tired and
harassed, as he generally did after " visi-
tations," for the Bishop was not always
pleasant upon these occasions.    Had he
seen anything of Madge?    Why, what a
foolish question!    How could he?    Was
there anything for supper?

When told that his daughter had not
slept at home last night, he turned a little
pale, but tushed! and pshawed! at Bell's

fears. The silly child was playing them some trick (Bell's own thought). She would come back before bedtime. He was yet supping with a good appetite, when a coastguard-man came in with Bell's nubia. He had found it caught in a furze bush half way down the cliff! Bell's worst fears are realised!

Every soul in that silent, stricken house loved her. It is no use trying to describe their consternation, their horror, their grief. Think of it! not yet nineteen, and gone suddenly to her account! To be married to-morrow, and dead to-day! The lithe little form which was to have worn a bridal dress when another sun rose, mangled by the cruel rocks! The sweet young face which was to have illumined a good man's life staring blankly at futurity,

*somewhere* in the silent sea ! Those who
can bend them o'er the dead and kiss the
cold casket of their lost jewel, ere they
consign it to the worm, have some poor
comfort.   These mourners had none.   The
spirit was gone from them—the body gone.
The sea would not give up its dead.   They
searched the beach below the cliff in vain.
They searched for miles—in vain.   Perhaps in days to come, they were told,
*something* might be cast up by the waves.
That was all the comfort that could be
given.   She was to have been married on
the morrow.   What should they say to
Fraser !   The Vicar was in his study
utterly prostrated with grief; would allow
no one to see or speak with him.   All
centred upon poor Bell.   His last bitter
words to her were, " Why did you let her
go out ?"   Poor Bell !   It was hard to

bear. She who had twined the nubia round her neck, and kissed her and bade her go out quick, in all tenderness and love —had almost driven her to her death; what can she say to Fraser?

Fraser's letter lies on the mantelpiece. Fraser himself is expected that night at his old quarters. She must telegraph and stop him. But where? Beckhampton, London—where? If not warned he will be at Laremouth in a few hours, and the news be blurted out by some inconsiderate —there were scores such—who would rush at him open-mouthed with the horror that awaited him. She must telegraph, and break it. She must open the letter just to see where he is—no more. His loving words should be sacred. They should rest with her, if her dear body be ever found; or be hidden for ever in the sea that hides her. Only the address is wanted. She opens the letter.

Can this be his hand ? so blurred, so incoherent ! No date, no address. She cannot help but read:

*" This is the fifth sheet I have began, but cannot tell you what I want in writing. If I could see you I could explain all. Our marriage must be postponed. Oh, my darling! love and trust me. Pray for me. I believe I am going mad.*

*" FRASER."*

The words swim before her eyes. For a time this burst of new misery overwhelms her. She cannot guess at what has happened. She can only stand there trembling and half dazed, reading the letter over and over again.

"Papa must see it," she says at last. "It will rouse him."

The Vicar has locked himself in the study, and will not even answer her knock. She goes round to the window, and sees him pacing up and down the room with his hands clasped behind his back. Very pale and worn is his face, but there is no mark of tears on it.

"Papa," she cries, disregarding his gesture of dismissal, "I must speak to you. Please let me in. Here is a letter from poor Fraser."

"From Fraser!" he exclaims, hastily unfastening the window. "Give it me. Let me see: from Fraser!"

He snatches it from her hand, and runs his eye quickly over it. Then he takes it to his writing-table, sits down, spreads it before him, and notes every word.

" There is some comfort in this," he says in a hollow voice.

" Comfort, papa !"

"You may come in, Bell.   No, never mind shutting the windows.   I only closed them to—to be alone.   It is so oppressive! And you have broken in upon me.   Leave them open."

" Oh, papa ! don't speak like that.   Do let us try to share each other's sorrow."

He is not attending to her.   His eyes are again on the letter.

" How   came   you   to   open   it ?"   he asks.

" To find out where to telegraph."

" There is no date."

" No."

" What   have   you   done   with   the   en-velope ?   Did you notice the post-mark ?"

" Here it is.   I never thought of that—

see, *London!* He had left Beckhampton, and was on his way."

"Yes ; he would have been here at nine o'clock to-night, if all had gone well."

"What can have happened to him ?"

"Ah ! that, perhaps, we shall never know. It is best that we should not inquire. My poor lost child has escaped a grievous shock. Think, Bell, what it would have cost her, if she had been alive, to read this letter ! It would have killed her. If she was to die, it is some comfort to feel that she died happy. As for Mr. Ellicott," continued the Vicar in quite a changed tone, "when your uncle arrives, he shall write to him at his club. I suppose they will know there where his new whim leads him."

"His whim, papa ?"

"His meanness and his treachery, then ;

that is plain enough," replies the Vicar, becoming violently excited all of an instant. "I've done with him. Postpone his marriage at a day's notice! Why, it would have disgraced us all!"

"Papa, dear," says Bell gravely, "you must not be hard on Fraser. God knows he has enough to bear in the calamity of which he is still ignorant, and he writes as if some terrible misfortune had happened."

"Pshaw! terrible misfortune! He has lost some money, or some forgotten vice has sprung up and confronted him. He can have no excuse for writing such a letter as that; and I have done with him. Never let me hear his name again; I hate the sound of it. But for him, my darling might have been alive to-day. What right had he to come here and win her

young heart, if he had some ' terrible misfortune ' hanging over him ?"

" You are *so* unjust ! I would stake
my life it is no fault of his," cries loyal
Bell.

" You generally follow your own
opinions," he replies fretfully. " You can
do so now ; only don't thrust them on me.
I desire that you do not mention Mr.
Ellicott's name to me again. On second
thoughts, I shall write to him myself when
my brain is a little clearer."

" My poor dear ! my poor dear !" sobs
Bell, throwing her arms round his neck.
" Cannot I comfort you ?"

" Comfort will come with time ; you
were right to rouse me, Bell. I must
rouse. There, there ! don't sob so, my
child ; we must bear up, if it be only to
go through the miserable form of receiving

the people who will be here to-night ; it
is too late to stop them."

" No, dear. I can write to Uncle Joe,
send it to the station, ask him to break
the news to Mr. Fluery and the rest, and
come on himself. We must have Uncle
Joe here, papa."

There was no time to be lost. She
wrote the letter then and there, and it
answered its purpose.

" The best thing you can do, my dear,"
says Uncle Joe to Bell next day, " is to
take the children and go home."

" What ! and leave poor papa alone ?"

" Your father always was a peculiar
man ; he likes to be alone. Some people
afflicted as he is find relief in talking over
even the most trivial details of their loss,
and speculating as to this or that which
may or may not have happened. He

don't. He will not say a word, and is angry or reproachful if one asks him questions. No, you cannot do any good to him here, Bell; and you may fret yourself quite ill. Take my advice; change the scene and its associations, and go back to your husband."

" You will stay ?"

" Yes. I shall consult your father's wishes by leaving him alone; but that won't prevent me from looking into this miserable affair a good deal closer than has been done yet."

" There's nothing that I have not told you."

" I'm not so sure of that."

" Oh, Uncle Joe ! confide in me. Have you any hope ?"

" No, dear, I have not. Nothing that I can do will bring back our sweet pet into life, but we can get much more certain than we are at present how she died."

"Who can tell? she was alone, poor child !"

"Was she?   That's the question."

"Good heavens! you cannot imagine—oh! that is impossible—that she was thrown over? she who had not an enemy in the world."

"She wore her pearls, my dear.   Many a man and woman has been murdered for less.   If we could find her we should know what to think on this head, but it won't do to wait, Bell.   We may never find her."

"What reason have you to suspect foul play?   Oh, please trust me, Uncle Joe.   I won't breathe a word, and I might help."

"Let us have Mason up, I have not seen him yet."

"I told you all he said."

"Yes, but I would rather have it from himself."

"Now, Mason," he said when that domestic appeared, "I want you to tell me exactly what you saw the night before last. Mind, not what you thought it was that you saw, but just what your eyes told you, and no more."

"Well, Sir Joseph," replied Mason, " I was in the pantry reading with a candle; and when the fog came so thick that I could not see no more, I shut the book, got up, and just as I did, somebody passed the window; and I thought——"

"No *thoughts*, Mason. Some one passed the window—well ?"

"Going towards the outside door of

master's study.   Now I knew Miss Margaret was out."

"How did you know that?"

"Why Lord, Sir Joseph, I saw her go, as I come back from smoking a pipe with William in the stable."

"Which way did she go?"

"Towards the cliff, where she walks most every day."

"What time was that?"

"About half-past nine."

"And what o'clock was it when that some one passed the pantry window?"

"An hour afterwards—or may be not so much.  It was eleven when I locked up."

"Did you see that some one go to the door of your master's study?"

"No, Sir Joseph."

"Did you hear anybody go upstairs?"

"No, Sir Joseph."

"Then when you told Mrs. De Gray that her sister had gone to bed, it was only because you *thought* that the some one who passed the window was she; and because you *thought* it was she going towards your master's study-door, you *thought* she had entered the house that way; and because you *thought* she had so entered the house, you stated positively that she had gone to bed. Is that so, Mason?"

Mason hung his head. "I could have taken my Bible oath—" he began.

"Yes, yes, yes; but see what comes of so much *thinking,* my good man. If you had been a little less confident in your own deductions you would have told Mrs. De Gray simply that you thought you had seen Miss Madge pass in the garden. Then inquiries would have been made;

your mistake would have been discovered, perhaps—who knows !—in time to save her. Let this be a lesson to you, Mason, to say what you know, and not what you *think* you know, when you talk about facts."

" You can take me, Sir Joseph, and you can chuck me over them cliffs, if——"

" I'm sure he meant well," interposes Bell.

" I never supposed he did not," said Uncle Joe; " I only want to impress upon him the difference between *I saw*, and *I supposed*. I've got what you saw, Mason; and now I'm coming to what you supposed. Why did you think that the figure which passed the pantry window at half-past nine o'clock was Miss Madge ?"

" Because she was out."

" No other reason ?"

" It was like her. She had that white thing of Mrs. De Gray's wrapped round her neck."

" Sure of that ?"

" Quite sure."

" Remember, it was night, and foggy. How can you be sure it was a white thing ?"

" Why, we've got it now, Sir Joseph ! Mrs. De Gray can tell you it is white."          .

" I see. You knew that Miss Madge wore something white about her neck ; and because the figure also had something round its neck, you conclude it was white ?"

" Yes, Sir Joseph."

" Well, we are on *supposes*, so I will not scold you. Now for facts again. You saw no face or colour ; it might have been a man, for anything you saw? Truth, Mason."

" There was no man about. William was in bed."

" It might have been a man," Uncle Joe repeats.

" If I had thought it was a man, I should have gone out and asked him what he was up to."

" It might have been a man, Mason, for all you saw."

" It might have been a cow," is wrung from the tortured butler.

" Were there any cows about ?"

" No, Sir Joseph."

" Then, according to your own logic, it could not have been a cow. That reply of yours was slightly impertinent, my man ; but never mind. Might it have been a man ?"

"Yes, it might," replies Mason, wiping his brows.

"I don't think it was quite so late as half-past nine when she went out," Bell remarks; "I heard the clock strike a good quarter of an hour after she left."

"Beg your pardon, ma'am," pleads Mason; "I heard it strike too, just as she opened the gate."

"Then she must have come back for something, and gone out again. I dare say you are right, Mason."

Kind-hearted Bell was sorry for the badgered butler, and threw him this little sop, for which he was duly grateful.

"I don't see what you have gained by all that cross-questioning," she observes, when the witness has left the room.

"Don't you, my dear?" replies her imperturbable uncle. " Then let me tell you. But a question or two first. Do you believe that Mason saw anything ?"

" Of course he saw something."

" Was it poor dear Madge ?"

" It could not have been any one else."

" Then you must believe that she came back *after* the fog had set in, and, knowing her danger, went deliberately to the cliff. Is that likely ?"

" Well, no."

" She had been away an hour already. It was half-past ten. Why didn't she come in ?"

" Then who could it have been ?" asks Bell.

" Ah ! That's what we want to know."

" What do you think yourself ?"

" That it certainly was not poor Madge."

" Papa says he did not hear or see any one."

" That does not prove that no one passed. I'm going to the village now, Bell, to find out what strangers were here the night before last."

" And you will see the police, won't you, Uncle Joe ?"

" No—o. I don't think I shall, my dear. I think we had better do without the police as much as possible. I've had four boats out since daylight searching for her," said the ex-diplomatist, drawing his hand across his eyes, " and some of them may have come back. Take my advice, and go to your husband by the express."

" Papa will think it so cruel."

"He will not think about it at all, child. He is quite stunned with grief. The kindest thing is to do as he bids us—leave him alone."

# CHAPTER V.

## THE FLOOD AT BECKHAMPTON.

O such flood as that which swept down the valley of the Beck on the 28th, 29th, and 30th of June had been known (I quote from the *Beckhampton Herald*) in the memory of the oldest inhabitant. It would have done Miller Hazeltine's heart good to have seen how fully his prophecy was fulfilled, and how fulfilment had revenged him upon his enemies, the steam mills. These had been established on the river-side, on purpose to intercept the grist on the way to its ancient natural grinder.    Rampageous Beck, as though siding with those who had nursed him in his weakness, and full of fury against these innovators, lapped away their foundations, and, bursting through their walls, left them a heap of red ruins, their tall chimney prostrate, their fires out, and their yard six feet under water, with half a hay-stack bobbing around it like a huge float.

With equal impartiality, the angry stream carried off the building materials which were to form the new bleaching works, and sent such portions of them as would float swimming down the widened current, for the boys to make rafts of when his rage was over.

At one time there were fears for the old

bridge ; and it really would have been as well if it had gone, for the massive but-tresses, and the *débris* they caught, pent back the flood, and sent it into the cellars, and even the ground floors, of the lower portion of the town, causing much misery and loss to people who could ill afford to suffer.

There was four feet of water in the meadows for miles round, dotted here and there with the thatched roofs of pig-sties and carcasses of dead sheep, which floated about mournfully. Cattle stood upon the higher grounds, made islands for the time, and filled the air with piteous lowings. Pigs stuck in hedge-rows squeaked and scrambled for dear life. Draggled hens that had had sufficient sense to take to the trees plumed themselves in a low-spirited way, and thought of their drowned chickens. The ducks alone had a fine time of it, and seemed to consider that what was an infliction upon all others, had been sent for their special benefit. I have known many highly respectable persons to go about as these ducks did, quacking over their neighbours' misfortunes.

The old bridge, as I have said, held its own, though the flood rose a foot above the crown of its highest arch. Not so the wall of Dr. Byng's Five's Court. That had been built by contract. About five o'clock on the afternoon of the 28th it collapsed like a house of cards, and then, and not till then, could the crowd which thronged the bridge see the extent of the overflow beyond.

" It's all over with the mill this time," said Mr. Pryor, thrusting his hands deep into his pockets, and setting his teeth. "Lucky there is no one there."

So saying, he went up to the old Hall to see if Fraser Ellicott had left yet.

"Where's the Squire?" he asked Mrs. Aymes, whom he found knitting in the housekeeper's room and evidently much out of humour.

"You should know best," she replied, "you was with him last. He never came home at all. I dare say he didn't spare the champagne."

"Well, he didn't; but if you mean to insinuate that he was the worse for it, Mrs. Aymes, you are mistaken. He was as sober as a judge when my son left him on the bridge, and he did not sleep at the Rose and Crown, for I was there half

an hour ago, and they would have told me
if he had."

"Then where is he ?   Oh, Mr. Pryor !
he couldn't have got caught by the flood ?"

"Not likely ; maybe he left by the last
train.   I'll ask at the station.   He did
talk about going by it so as to have half a
day in London, to get some things he
wanted for his sweetheart."

"He might have told me so," said the
housekeeper reproachfully.   "I sat up half
the night waiting for him."

"Gentlemen in love are often very inconsiderate," pleaded Pryor.   "He'll have
to consider a good many now.   We must get
up a subscription for all those poor people
who are drowned out of their homes, and
he should head it."

"Can't you put down his name for him,
Mr. Pryor ?"

"Yes, but that isn't the same thing as putting it down himself, you know. He isn't as popular as he ought to be, thanks to that young Wybert; and this would have been a fine opportunity for him to come out handsomely. I wish to goodness he had stayed. It would have taken a heap of responsibility off my shoulders, and now I suppose we shan't catch him for months."

"Is there much damage done, Mr. Pryor?"

"A good deal, I am afraid, though it hasn't reached our property—except the Mill. That's gone."

"Hazeltine's Mill!" exclaimed the housekeeper.

"Sure to be. It was touch and go with it last flood, and that didn't come so high by five inches. Good job for the Hazeltines that they left in time, and that girl may thank her stars that the Squire sent her here."

Mrs. Aymes gave a sudden cry, and dropped her knitting.

"She isn't here," she gasped. "She ran away last night."

"Ran away?"

"Yes, ran away; she was half crazy, I think. No woman in her senses would have carried on as she did. Abused Master Fraser, and refused his service, and—and oh, Mr. Pryor! if she went back to the Mill!"

"What time did she leave?"

"I don't know; she was asleep when I last saw her. That was about five o'clock; I thought she was quite tired out, and so I left her. It was after nine when I found she had run away. What is to be done?"

" If she went to the Mill, little more than to look for her body, I am afraid," Pryor replied.

" But you're not sure the Mill is down."

" I would not give you a brass sixpence for it.  The last time the Beck rose, old Hazeltine told me that he stood by all night with pick and spade ready to cut the dam as the only way to save the house. He knew his risk better than any man in the valley.  If the water had come up another hand's breadth he would have cut. There is no one there to do so now, and I tell you the flood is more than a hand's breadth higher than it was then."

" But why not go and make *sure?*" pleaded Mrs. Aymes, wringing her hands.

" It's easy to say go and make sure ; but how ? the paths are all under water; so is the road.  We've no boats, and if we had, who could manage one in such a rush? It would be upset before you knew where you were."

"Don't tell me, Mr. Pryor, that there is no getting anywhere to see. The Mill-house is big enough to be seen, I hope, if it's standing."

"Ah, *if.*"

"I've no patience with such 'ifs,'" cried the old lady, starting up. "I'll go myself. The girl hasn't behaved well to me, but I won't stand by and let her be drowned like a blind kitten; and so I tell you, Mr. Pryor. I reckon the water ain't so high but what a horse and cart can go round by Stowe Lane."

"A good thought," said the agent, brightening up; "anyhow we can *see*, as you say, from that side. I'll go directly. Sit down, Mrs. Aymes. Depend upon me that what can be done shall be done. After all perhaps she did not go home. It's best to hope she didn't."

He was as good as his word. He got a waggon—the highest he could find—and four horses, and drove round by Stowe Lane, a circuit of seven miles, flanking the flood. From the point of vantage suggested by Mrs. Aymes, he saw with surprise and delight that the old Mill, like the old bridge, had held its own. There it stood, splitting the flood into the form of a letter

# Y,

with the water lapping the bricks of its yard up to within a stone's throw of the house porch !

"Bravo ! old Mill," shouted Pryor. " Look here, Benson " (this to his driver), " the water has made a way for itself just

exactly where Mr. Hazeltine said we ought
to have a safety-sluice ; and where I would
have had one made, but for Mrs. Banfield's
obstinacy. She has caught it now.
Wouldn't let us run a three-foot ditch
down the side of her meadow, and now
look there." He pointed his stick to where
a branch of my Y—brown, rapid and deep—
swirled and curdled along, sixty yards wide.
Indeed the main body of the flood appeared
to be going down that way. On the other
side—the side which the river took in its
natural course—the stream was broader,
but shallow, and Pryor, descending the hill
from Stowe Lane, found that he could
advance a considerable way before the
water was up to the chests of his horses.
This brought him within speaking distance
of the Mill-house, and at his first shout, a
woman—whom he had not yet observed,

who had been sitting with her face buried in her hands, rocking herself to and fro on the frame of the main sluices—sprang up and ran for the open door as a rabbit for its hole. At his second call (this time by name) she stopped, closed the door and locked it. Then she walked slowly to the verge of the flood, and asked what they wanted.

"What do I want?" repeated Pryor, with a laugh. "It seems to me that what *you* want is the question just now. Can I get any nearer, do you think?" He is standing up in the waggon trying to make out where he is by the lines of the hedges, and other land-marks. But flood, like fog, is very deceptive. The leaders of his team have turned round, as though they smelt deep water. Kate Vane's reply shows that they are wiser than their drivers.

"No," she says; "you are on the top of

the slope leading down to the road. There is ten feet of water where that tree is floating."

"How far could you wade from your side without getting out of your depth ?"

"Not far."

"Can you get half way ?"

"No, nor a quarter," Kate replied.

"The deuce!" mutters Pryor. A quarter of the way would not even bring her to the edge of where the water ran curdling deep and reddened by the marl banks of the road ; and this (counting in the slope) was at least twelve yards wide. "Have you any rope in the Mill ?" he shouted after a little consideration.

"I dare say there is," she replied ; " do you want some ?"

"You seem to take it mighty coolly !

How do you think you are going to get across ?"

" I don't want to get across."

" Nonsense, girl ! You don't know the risks you are running. Get a long rope ; float one end of it over here, and we will drag you across. Better a ducking than a drowning, any day."

" Better a dry skin than either," Kate answered him. " Thank you very much, Mr. Pryor. It was very kind of you to come after me, but really I prefer to remain where I am. If I had wanted to go, I could have left last night."

" I tell you it is not safe," said Pryor, vexed at her coolness after all his trouble. " The foundations of the house may be undermined. It may fall in at any moment. I hear you and Mrs. Aymes had some fuss. Never mind that. You need not go to the Hall. We'll take care of you for a day or two. Only look sharp and get the rope."

" There is no danger," she replied calmly, not moving an inch.

" I have heard that you are headstrong and self-opinionated," he snapped, for he was getting angry; "but I did not expect you to set your judgment against mine."

" I have no opinion of my own, Mr. Pryor," the girl replied. " I only act upon that of one who knows better than both of us."

" Who's that ?"

" My uncle."

" Now let me tell you this, Kate Vane ; your uncle would not have stayed an hour in that house with the water above the sluices—unless——"

" Yes—unless ?"

" Unless the dam by the corner of Banfield's meadow were cut."

Kate turned and pointed to where the
full strength of the flood was rushing ; with
a gesture half of triumph, and half a
sneer.

" Ah," replied the agent, " it has burst
now ; but think of the pressure there was
on the house before it gave way !"

" There was no pressure," said Kate
quietly. " When the river came up to the
mark uncle made two years ago, I cut the
bank."

" You !" cried Pryor.

" Why not ? A few spadefuls dug out,
sent the water to find its own way. It did
the rest for itself."

" Then you have saved the property !
you're a fine brave girl," Pryor shouted,
with genuine admiration.

A shrug of her shoulders and a curl of her lip was all the reply he got.

"Only think of that!" he went on, turning to his driver. "Watched; and cut the dam. Only a few spadefuls, eh? Egad! every one of them is a thousand pounds in the Squire's pocket. They can call her what they like, but she don't want for pluck."

"She will for wittels though, if she stops," was the driver's observation, for he was a practical man.

"That's so," said Pryor. "Holloa! Miss Vane; don't go in yet. How are you off for supplies?"

"I have everything I want, thank you, sir."

"Sure of that? because we shall have rafts and boats out by to-morrow, and can send you anything you want."

" Please don't send," she replied
quickly; "there are many, I dare say,
who want aid much more than I do. I
have all I shall require for the next
fortnight—except fresh meat; and I can
get on very well without that. Indeed,
Mr. Pryor, I would much rather you did
not send, but I thank you all the same."

" You'll be very lonely."

" I have to get accustomed to that."

" There will be fever, sure, when the
flood goes down—so much evaporation and
dead things about."

She shuddered all over.

" Where would the flood take any—any
dead things ?" she asked.

" Well, any that kept straight in the
stream would go down to the sea, but they
generally get caught in hedges; and left
dry here and there."

" Have you seen any ?"

" No ; we came by the road.  I don't think you'll stop here very long.  If you change your mind, hang a sheet out of that window, and I'll send a boy every day as far as Highstone Hill, to see if your signal is out."

" You are very kind.  That will do capitally.  If I want anything I will signal, and if I don't no one need trouble himself about me.  Is that agreed ?"

" Certainly."

" Will you tell Mrs. Aymes when you see her, that I did not run away from *her ?*"

" I will.  Anything else ?"

" No ; good-evening, Mr. Pryor, and a pleasant journey home.  Mind how you turn."

After a good deal of splashing and snorting the waggon was turned, and went its way back to Beckhampton.

"What's that black thing in the hedge?" said Mr. Pryor, as they were nearing the dry land.

"Looks like a dead chicken," said the driver.

"Why it's a hat, man! Can you reach it with your whip?"

"Noa."

"Take off your shoes and stockings, and go in after it. You won't get beyond knee deep," said Pryor.

"Ay, but will it be mine if I get it?" asked practical Benson.

"I don't suppose any one will dispute it with you—*I* won't. Picking it up will be worth something to you anyhow, if it's only a glass of ale."

25—2

"Here goes then," said the man.

Two minutes afterwards he was shaking the wet out of an excellent London-made hat which, as good fortune would have it, fitted him exactly. Better still, although the finding was chronicled in the *Herald* (together with an account of the "admirable presence of mind evinced by Miss Kate Vane"), no one claimed it, and practical Mr. Benson wore it to church in triumph.

## CHAPTER VI.

### THE AWFUL CATASTROPHE AT LAREMOUTH.

BY this time poor Madge's fate is public property. The local papers give it to the world under sensational headings : " AWFUL CATASTROPHE AT LAREMOUTH ! ! A YOUNG LADY FALLS FROM THE CLIFFS IN A FOG ! !" Even the great London dailies find a corner for the news. Wherever Fraser Ellicott may be, or whatever he is doing, it must reach him.

Bell has come back to town, and is prostrated by all she has gone through. As soon as she can crawl out of her room, she goes in search of Fraser. He is not at his club ; he has not been at his lodgings since he returned from Beckhampton. The yacht, sent to Dover to embark the bride and bridegroom, has sailed—no one knows whither. Uncle Joe has promised to telegraph and write whatever may happen, and he has no news of Fraser. In one of his letters he writes :

" It is not likely that we shall hear from him after such a letter as your father wrote. He cannot, or will not, understand that poor Madge's fate and Fraser's misfortune (whatever it may be) are two distinct and separate things, and takes the former as the consequence of the latter. If he had jilted her, and she had (which God forbid!)

flung herself from the cliff, your father could not have written more bitterly."

Had Fraser received this letter ? If not, it must be intercepted. Bell thinks she can do so by writing for it to his club in his name—a benevolent forgery, for which she may be forgiven. There are no letters for Mr. Ellicott.

"Then he has received it," she sighs. "Poor Fraser !"

Uncle Joe has declined to investigate the reasons which might have led to a postponement of the wedding, if Madge had not gone out that night.

"One thing at a time, my dear," he says to Bell, as she is leaving Laremouth. "I've got to clear up all about poor Madge first ; and then we'll see."

Bell cannot wait to see. If it were a money trouble, the Right Honourable

Temple Fluery would know. The Right Honourable Temple Fluery is not aware that Mr. Ellicott's affairs are embarrassed in any way, and begs to refer Mrs. De Gray to the family attorney, Mr. Pryor, of Beckhampton. Nor is this gentleman any wiser. His client had entertained his friends on his birthday, and was in excellent health and spirits. He left late that night for London.

"Then he has gone abroad with his sorrow," muses Bell. "Poor Fraser!"

Several strangers had arrived from land or sea at Laremouth on the night of the 28th of June, but one and all were fully able to account for themselves, except a small and remarkably stupid boy, named Peter Brown, who had come from an inland town to be bound 'prentice to his uncle, a sailmaker. This urchin ought to have been at his new home by nine o'clock at the latest, and he was not housed till after ten. He would not say what he had been doing, nor would he account for one half-crown and small change for another, less one and sevenpence, which was discovered in his pocket.

Being a sort of culprit, he is taken before Uncle Joe, who admits at once that he cannot be the same one who passed the pantry window, as his hand would barely reach the sill. Nevertheless, to satisfy the sailmaker, who has taken an active part in the search for poor Madge, and is uneasy about the mysterious wealth of his nephew, Uncle Joe examines that capitalist, and elicits the following facts :

As he was tramping from the station, he was overtaken by a gentleman on horseback, who dismounted near the

Vicarage, gave him a letter, and told him to go in there, ask for Miss Marston, and give it into her own hands. If he came back with her reply, which was to be *yes* or *no*, he was to have five shillings. He obeyed; and whilst waiting in the road, thinking how he was to do his errand, a young lady came out. He asked her if Miss Marston was at home, and she said she was Miss Marston. Then he gave her the letter. She took it back with her into the hall, and read it under the lamp. Then she " staggered like " into a chair, and sat there a good bit, with the letter in her lap. At last she came out again, told him to tell the gentleman *yes*, and walked away.

In what direction? He didn't know.

What was the gentleman like? Well, he was like a gentleman.

Had he ever seen him before ?   No.

Should he know him again ?   Yes, he would.

" How was he dressed ?"

" He had on one of them petticut coats, wi' a night-cap to 't."   (Evidently an Ulster.)

" What ! on a hot night like that ?"

" Yes, he had ; and the cap thing almost covered his face."

Had he (the boy) been through the Vicar's garden ?   No.

" Did the gentleman go in there ?"

" No ; as soon as he gi' me the money, he rode off."

" After the young lady ?"

The boy could not say what he was after.

" But did he go the same way ?"

" No ; he went t'other way."

" Back again towards the station ?"

" Yes."

" What o'clock was it ?"

" Couldn't say."

" Was there any fog ?"

" No ; it was bright enough then."

Here was a discovery ! What did it mean ? Could it be that Fraser, impatient of the post's delay, or anxious in a calmer moment to undo the effect of his incoherent scrawl, had written more fully to Madge by a messenger, explaining what his reasons for postponing their marriage were, and begging her to put it off on some excuse ? This might have been what she was to say *yes* or *no* to—this what made her stagger to a chair, as the boy had described—this, what had blinded and bewildered her more than the fog ; made head swim and foot fail at her thinking-place on the cliff. Or

—Good God ! could she in grief and des-
pair— A cold shudder ran to the old man's
heart as the thought arose. It was the
one he had scouted in his letter to Bell.
"Oh no : good little Madge ! Impossible!
He never could be such a villain as that ;
or she so weak. She would have borne
her burden, though it broke her heart,"
he muses.

But if the messenger rode back to the
station, *his* could not have been the figure
which passed Mason's window. Suppose
he had not ridden back ! That could
easily be proved. There was a toll-bar
about half way—the keeper would know.
This worthy remembered having opened
the gate for a man on horseback wearing a
big coat.

"I minded the coat," he said, "'cause
it worn't a night for putting *on* a

coat. I was a-sweating in my shirt-sleeves."

" Did the man return ?"

" No, that he didn't. There worn't no saddle 'oss through again that night."

" A hired horse is an easy thing to trace," thought Uncle Joe. " I think I have that gentleman, and shall take off his coat."

The horse he found without much difficulty. It had been hired at the Livery Stable at the station, by a gentleman who paid for it in advance, and it had come back—by itself. Who let it to the gentleman ? Bill Sidebottom. Ah ! Uncle Joe would like to have a few moments' conversation with Bill. So would the Livery Stable-keeper ; for Bill's month was up, and he had left the day before without accounting for the sovereign that gentleman had paid him. It is unnecessary to say that Mr. Sidebottom did not leave any address.

So the messenger must have skirted the toll-bar by some by-path, and sent his horse to find his own way back. Why? Because he did not want to be traced. Why should an honest messenger shirk like this? *Was* he an honest messenger? or a messenger at all? Uncle Joe was puzzled. Might he not have doubled back. when he left the boy, followed Madge to the cliff and— But where was the motive? To rob her? How should a stranger know that the poor girl had put on her pretty wedding present! Again, if he had thrust her from the cliff, or she had fallen in a struggle with him; she would have cried out. Anyhow he would not have been so mad as to come to the Vicarage afterwards, and risk surprise and arrest. The more the mystery was examined, the darker it became ; and the darker it became, the more it put Uncle Joe upon his metal.

" I'll be damned if I don't get to the bottom of it," growled Uncle Joe. Not having a reading order for Heaven's chancery, as some good people have, I am unable to inform you if this gentleman is on the wrong side of its books.

The four boats returned fruitless from their dismal voyage. The face of the cliff was searched and searched again for some further relic of the lost girl. Not a cranny that a sailor could stand in, or be swung to by a rope, was left unexamined. Some loose stones had fallen here and there— that was all. The tide had been up on the beach beneath soon after midnight, and would have washed away all marks of the horrid fall. She must have gone down almost straight — a clean drop of two hundred feet ! if she had gone over where Bell's nubia was found. There were no traces of footsteps on the tough close turf above. Oh me ! It was hard to stand there amidst so many silent witnesses, and to know nothing.

The boy's story sets people talking. If Uncle Joe had only known what was to be disclosed, you may be sure that it would not have been told in public. It came out bit by bit; and the mischief was done before mischief was suspected. Heretofore the examination had been conducted by variations upon a blustering " *You* tell me what you've been up to !" and a blubbering " *You* gi' me back my money !" Uncle Joe took the delinquent between his knees, patted him on the head, bade him not be afraid but tell the truth like a good boy, and he should have his money. Thus cajoled, out it all came. There was no stopping in the middle. Half a dozen of the worst gossips heard it. The young man from the *Battleville Mercury,* who was there collecting items of the *awful catastrophy,* got hold of it and its author, and worked them both up. The idea which Uncle Joe would not even take into consideration ran glibly from tongue to tongue. That mysterious horseman had brought Miss Marston bad news from her sweetheart, and she had thrown herself over the cliff! Mason, who is a leaky vessel by nature, and much pumped, especially by the young man from the *Mercury,* lets out an incident which confirms this theory.

"I didn't think nothing of it at the

time," he explains, "but it does look mighty odd now—don't it ?"

This " it " was the conduct of Mrs. De Gray at the Vicar's window.

" I'll take my Bible oath," protested Mason, "that the letter she had in her hand was the one as came that morning for Miss Madge, and it was in his" (meaning Fraser's) "writing. Why there was sometimes two on 'em a day — always one ! *I* know his writing. And it worn't pleasant news neither. She was as pale as a ghost, and when he " (meaning the Vicar) "see it, he let her in. He wouldn't let her in, or nobody before."

The gossips like Madge, but love scandal more. And they do not love the Vicar in the least. He preaches over their heads, he takes no interest in their affairs, he has pinched several of them severely in his

26—2

impecunious days, and now he gets his supplies from Battleville! They resent a movement amongst the better disposed to hush it up, for the Vicar's sake. "Why should it be hushed up? If she'd ha' bin a poor gal would he a hushed it up?" is asked; and some instances in which the Vicar has been hard upon poor girls' sins are freely quoted. "They may say what they like," sums up old Mrs. Withers. "She knew them cliffs by heart; every stone on 'em. I've seen her there day after day, and night after night. Fog or no fog, she could a walked along 'em blindfold. Tell me she slipped? It's ridiculous!"

The Vicar, who persists in locking himself up and refusing to speak to any one, is feverishly anxious to read what is printed about him and his loss. He is furious with Uncle Joe for keeping the newspapers away from him, as was done at first with the kindest intentions. He insists upon seeing them all, and even orders the *Beckhampton Gazette* in case there might be something published there. This journal has no young man on the spot, and supplies the curiosity of its readers by means of paste and scissors. It thus affords a summary of news and comments on news ; and this is perhaps why Mr. Marston reads it first of all. He does not combat the cruel scandal that his child has committed suicide, because he is spared that. He takes no notice of Uncle Joe's discoveries and speculations, when at last he consents to see him, except to pho-pho! the theory of foul play. "Mason is an idiot," he says. "Who could come through the garden at that time of night ?

It must have been a bat or an owl flutter-
ing by the window."

"You forget the boy's statement," Uncle
Joe replies.

" I do not believe one word of it. The
young rascal stole the money, and got up that
cock and a bull story to excuse himself."

" I suppose he invented the man on
horseback also?" observes Uncle Joe dryly.

"Nonsense about your man on horseback!" peevishly retorts the Vicar. " He
came here and he went back again. What
has that to do with it? You run down
the police for forming theories, and then
fitting evidence to them, but you do the
very same thing yourself. If you knew
that fellow at the toll-bar as well as I do,
you'd not value his oath a sixpence. He
was asleep when your man on horseback
went back. Why he might have been the

inspecting officer of the coastguard come on the sly to see if the men were at their duty! He often does."

" Perhaps you can account for his horse coming home without him ?"

" Who says his horse came home without him ?"

" Well, it was found saddled and bridled at the gate when they got up in the morning."

" Exactly! And what would you do yourself if you came back late at night to a place like that, on a hired horse, and there was no one up to receive it. Take it to bed with you? I should hitch it outside the stable door—as probably your mysterious man did, and go about my business."

" That is certainly one way of regarding it," mused Uncle Joe.

" And the most reasonable one. Do we

live in the atmosphere of a French romance, or in a dull English village? You have been very kind and considerate to me, brother Joseph, in my sore distress," he continued, taking the Baronet's hand and pressing it. "Do me one more kindness. Throw up this fancy of yours—for it is only a fancy. The *best* thing, in every sense of the word, that we can do for my poor child, is let her be forgotten. Yes, it sounds unkind; but, believe me, it is the right thing to do for her sake and—and for ours. In this view, I have arranged with a friend near London to exchange duties till Christmas—perhaps we shall exchange altogether—I could not live alone in this dismal place. I shall probably leave next Monday; and when the new clergyman arrives, these idiots will have something else to chatter about."

Thus is the subject diverted, and Uncle Joe finds that he has made no promise to throw up his fancy. He finds it a little shaken by the Vicar's argument. The most suspicious part of the mysterious horseman's conduct may be explained as he suggested ; but enough remains to call for further inquiry. As for poor Madge, the mischief is done. Idle tongues can say no worse of her than is already said. Uncle Joe utterly disagrees with his brother-in-law on this head, but does so in silence. " Going to leave on Monday," he muses, " that's a hint to me. Very well ; I'll take it. There's nothing more to do here except to find some clue to that ostler; people don't hire horses with their head and faces muffled up. If I could only get hold of Mr. William Sidebottom, I have an idea that I should see daylight."

He has kept his promise to Bell. "If you pick each incident to pieces by itself as your father does," he writes, "there is not much to go upon. Put them all together, and there is enough to counterbalance the spiteful, wicked charge made against poor Madge. I believe the boy, for he is far too stupid to invent such a story. Besides, do you remember the difference you and Mason had about the time when she left the house? He says it was half-past nine; you, that the clock struck some time after she had left. Does not this seem to corroborate the boy's story that she came back into the hall and remained there reading the letter, and making up her mind about it, till Mason saw her start out again? Mason says that he did not see the boy; but the boy now admits that he saw Mason, and dodged him. I believe the boy, and hope to see you on Saturday, to talk this over, as I shall leave to-morrow, and look up Sidebottom on the way. I may have to go to Battleville, etc., etc.

" P.S.—*Very important.* Old Probert, your father's clerk, found the gate leading to the churchyard open on the morning of the 29th. The stupid creature says he didn't think it mattered, as an excuse for not mentioning it before. Bats and owls do not open gates.

" J. B."

# CHAPTER VII.

## BILL "THE ROPER."

HE station which, in railway parlance, "served" Laremouth, was a junction where the road, which had its terminus at Battleville, joined the main South-Coast line—a spot for shuntings and taking tickets, where folks bound for the fashionable watering-place strapped up their rugs, or shook the dust from their gowns, and said, "Here we are!" where those on the other track asked, "Where are we?" and wondered why the train should stop so soon; a "jumping-off place," as our American cousins would call it, on the downs, with not a house in sight.

The name of the contractor for that part of the works was Ramsden; so, as it had to be given a name, it figures in Bradshaw as Ramsden Junction, and its inn (built by a speculator long since bankrupt) is known as the Ramsden Arms. Here farmers bound for market left their carts and gigs and took the rail, and a glass of something short in winter to keep out the cold, and of something long in hot weather to lay the dust.

Passengers for Laremouth and its vicinity hired flies; and in the hunting season inveterate Nimrods, who despised the flesh-pots of Battleville, put up their

horses, and devoted themselves to their
sport in an undiluted atmosphere of stable.
When hounds met the Ramsden Arms
was busy enough ; in the month of June
it was a wilderness that did not even howl.

Here Mr. William Sidebottom had
served for one month, and I regret to say
had not given satisfaction.   He was (*teste*
his defrauded employer) very cheeky, had
a proclivity to gin and an incapacity for
accounts, evinced before he pocketed that
sovereign for the hire of a horse he had
no business to let.   For this he had "got
the sack."   The question now was, where
he had gone with that emblem of
discharge ?   To Battleville on the west ?
to Pavilionborough on the east ? to London, Oxford, or Jericho—where ?   If there
had been an echo at Ramsden Junction, it
would no doubt have made the usual satis-

factory reply. From the landlord of the
Ramsden Arms no reply whatever was to
be had ; he was a sulky man, and sulked.
The barmaid tossed her head, and observed
that " them as come after such as him, had
better go to such as him for information."

Uncle Joe took off his hat, and thanked
her politely (for it was an excellent hint),
to her no small surprise.

" I'll go to the station," mused Uncle
Joe, " and pick out the most disreputable
creature I can find."

After due search and deliberation, his
choice fell on the lamp-trimmer. He was
feeble, he was greasy ; there was water in
his eye and grog-blossoms on his nose.
When the visitor the authorities of the
Ramsden Arms had snubbed announced
his name and rank, ordered dinner in a
private room, and after his repast sent for

that lamp-trimmer, mine host was struck
"all of a heap." When, half an hour
afterwards, the Baronet paid his bill and
again expressed his obligations to the lady
at the bar for her very kind assistance,
that damsel fell flop into a chair, and
loudly declared that she " *never !*"

In the meantime, the following conversation had taken place :

" Now, my man," Uncle Joe commenced,
" I want to find Bill Sidebottom. There's
a sovereign for you if you tell me where,
and there's five for him if he answers me
half a dozen questions. Name your
liquor, and if you mean business let's have
it."

The lamp-man named rum. He had
named rum, with the assistance of a pre-
paratory half-crown, bestowed at the com-
mencement of this acquaintance, twice

already. He named it again, and he got it. Business he postponed till he had gulped the last drop. It is well to make the best of the good things that be whilst they are—in the tumbler.

"There's a many folks after Bill," began the lamp-man.

"Name them."

"Well, *him,*" with a jerk of his greasy thumb in the direction of where the land lord might be, "to begin with."

"He has a tongue, I suppose, and can ask for himself. Who else?"

"Folks as has got things agin him."

"What does that matter to me? I have not got anything against him."

"Sure?"

"Quite sure. I've got five pounds for him—that's all."

"Well, I don't know where he is."

"Where did he go that night?" Uncle Joe asks.

"What night?"

"The night of the 28th of June, or the morning of the 29th? Come, you know. It's worth a sovereign to say."

"No harm to Bill?" pleads the lamp-man.

"Five sovereigns to Bill. Out with it."

"He went to London by the goods train along with Charley Watson."

"And who, pray, is Charley Watson?"

"The stoker. He wore a pal of his, like me."

"And where may Charley Watson live?"

"In London."

"London is a big place."

"You ain't promised anything for Charley," replies the lampman, with a tipsy leer of his rum-dimmed eyes.

" No, and I'm not going to," replied Uncle Joe. " I want Bill, not Charley. If I find him through his pal, as you call him, or if you give me reasonable prospects that I shall do so, it will be all the same for you."

" Charley lives somewhere back of the Victoria Station."

" Is that the nearest you can get to it ?"

" Number nine, Alma Terrace, off Theobald's Row. I lived next door there myself when I was a——

" A what ?"

" Well, a guard," the lamp-man answered doggedly.

" Oh ! you were a guard once, were you ? Have another glass of rum ?"

The lamp-man did not drink this one so quickly. He became gratified for favours

27—2

to come, and eloquent upon the anger, hatred, and malice of the traffic manager, who had reduced him from his former high estate " for nothink."

" But there was a fuss, you know," said Uncle Joe, shaking his head at him, not severely.   " There was something wrong ?"

"How was I to know he was up to anything wrong ?" demanded the lamp-man.

" He ? who was he ?"

" Why, Bill."

" Ah, indeed.   I'm sorry for that.   It was he who led you into it then ?"

" I didn't go in at all.   He persuaded me to lend him the key, and went in him-self," whimpered the lamp-man.

" And what did he do when he went in ?"

" That's none of my business."

" Of course not ; you weren't there at all. But what did they *say* he did ?"

" They say he *got at her.*"

" Poor thing, poor thing !" said sympathising Uncle Joe. " Do you think you could manage another glass ?"

The lamp-man thought he could.

" You did not mention her name," insinuates Uncle Joe, lighting a cigar. " You'll excuse my smoking. Your oil is rather strong, isn't it ? Would you like one ? yes, I think it might be better if you were to smoke. Her name was—?"

" Penelope."

" Penelope, what ?"

" Penelope nothink—don't you know ? She was favourite for the Muscatel Stakes in 1870."

" Oh ! a horse !"

" No, a mare ; and a good un too."

" I see.  And so he borrowed your key and went in and got at her.  What happened ?"

" *She didn't win them stakes,*" said the lamp-man with transparent mystery.

" She might not have won anyhow," Uncle Joe suggests.

" No more she mightn't," exclaims the lamp-man ; " and yet they discharged me."

" What was done to Bill ?"

" Nothing.  They couldn't prove nothing, and they can't prove nothing, and I snaps my fingers in their faces, I do," said the lamp-man, trying to suit the action to the word, but his fingers were too greasy to snap.  " And Bill, he's all right too, or I wouldn't be talking like this—no, not for all the gold in the bank !  They couldn't prove nothing ; but he'd bin up before the stewards for roping, and so——"

" He was a jockey then ?"

" Lord ! haven't you ever heard tell of Bill ' the Roper?' "

" I cannot say that I have."

" Well, that's him. He was blowed upon a'ready, and that blowed upon him more. No racing stable would have him, and so he come here."

" It was very kind of you to remain his friend," observes the questioner, " after he had got you into such a scrape. It does you great credit, Mr.—Mr.——"

" Thomas is my name," said the lamp-man.

" Mr. Thomas ; yes. Many would not have kept up with him, but sports-men stick together, don't they, Mr. Thomas ?"

" They've got to," replied the lamp-man decisively.

" I dare say you used to make your little bets ?"

" Ay, and do now ; but they're mighty little."

" You had your money on the Muscatel Stakes in 1870, I'll be bound ?"

" Of course I did."

" But not on Penelope, ha, ha !" laughed Uncle Joe.

" Haw ! haw ! haw !" roared the lamp-man. " That's a good un ! No, no, not on Penelope. There was a good many as won money on that race—not on Penelope; oh no !"

" Now how much might Bill have won ?"

" He got five—hun—dred—pound," said Mr. Thomas, who was now all under the influence of rum, and a particularly strong cigar. " Five—-hun—dred—pound, and

his gal robbed him of every shilling! She
was a bad lot, but such a topper! She
wore down here at Battleville wi' a swell
last season. I knowed her. Honourable
Mrs. Bletchingly, if you please! All
silks and satins, and a pair of thorough-
breds in a mail phaeton! What a game
for Sally Sidebottom to be sure."

"It is a pity your pal Bill wasn't here
then. Perhaps she might have restored
part of the money."

"That's wot he's up to now— Don't
you see?" said the lamp-man in a tone of
tipsy triumph, drawing closer to his
host.

"I think I could see as well a little
farther off," said Uncle Joe, retiring his
chair. "So he has gone to hunt up the
fair Sally—I beg her pardon, the Honourable Mrs. Bletchingly."

"That's it. D—— me but you're a smart one !"

"But why did not he hunt her up before, if she was at Battleville last season ?"

"He didn't know that."

"But you could have told him."

"Why I never see him for two years, till I come here a fortnight ago !" explained the lamp-man.

Uncle Joe sat silent for some minutes digesting this information. Then he asked if Mr. Charley Watson had anything to do with "getting at" Penelope, and was informed that he was not in that game. They used to get drunk together — Charley's "days off." He was to have a ten-pun' note for taking Bill up on his "en-gine," if that gentleman got his rights.

" So ye see, mister," hiccupped the lamp-man now fairly (some may think *un-fairly*) drunk, " he's no call for your rubbishy five (hic) pounds—he hasn't. He (hic) 'ull be a gen'leman—he will. Where's my sov'."

The séance ended by Mr. Thomas falling into a stertorous slumber, in which happy state Sir Joseph left him, and proceeded to astonish the bar-maiden as already recorded. •

" So," he said as he closed his pocket-book in the London express, " I have London to search in, with a drunken stoker and the Honourable Mrs. Bletchingly for guides ! I think I have heard of that lady. Will she introduce me to Bill ' the Roper ?' If she thought that I could introduce him to the Honourable Mr. Bletchingly, perhaps she would."

It is too late to visit Mr. Charles
Watson that night, and when Uncle Joe
calls at Alma Terrace the following day,
he finds that the stoker is " on the road."
Upon inquiry for Bill " the Roper," but
not by that name, he is informed that he
has behaved shameful.  His informant is
Mrs. Watson; a pale, worn-out woman
engaged at a washing-tub, with four small
children howling in four different keys
around her.  Mr. Sidebottom had lived on
them for a week, borrowed ten shillings,
got a lot of money, and—as Mrs. W. indignantly expressed herself — " hooked
it."

" He has found out his old love," said
Sir Joseph Balderson to Uncle Joe.  " So
long as supplies come from that quarter,
he will not mind me.  Couldn't the supplies be stopped ?"

This requires reflection. In the meantime he reports progress to Bell.

" I am glad papa is going to leave that
wretched place," she says. "How I do
detest it ! If it were not for that dear
Jessie Westwood—Oh ! you can't think
how good she has been—I wish the sea
would come up and sweep it all away, I
do, Uncle Joe ! How dare they think my
poor sweet innocent darling would commit
suicide ! They ought to be flogged."
Bell's judgments are inconsistent, as
angry people's judgments will be.

" Was she in good spirits that night ?"
asked Uncle Joe after a pause.

" Not very. She was nervous and over-
wrought, poor child ! Talked about disappointments in love, and asked me if
men got over them easily. I thought
since that she must have had some idea

that that creature Mr. Wybert cared for her."

" Indeed !"

" Yes, and that she was sorry for him."

" But you don't suppose he did ?"

" Oh dear no. It was just a girl's notion. She was so kind-hearted."

"That she was." And then they compared notes how she had tried to make up for the Vicar's coldness towards Mr. Wybert; and so, of course, it came out that Madge had met him " by accident " whilst she was in London.

" I suppose he is at Barbadoes by this time ?" said Bell. " I never liked him, but I must confess I think papa has behaved badly. He might have liked Fraser ever so, without throwing the other so completely overboard."

" Your father is a peculiar man, my

dear," says her uncle. " He has only one
idea at a time, and he works it to death.
He is furious with poor Fraser now."

" What *can* have happened to him ?"
Bell sighs.

" Goodness only knows all ! What we
know is bad enough."

" Poor fellow ! I wish he could know
one foolish idea she had. She thought
that life with him promised too much hap-
piness. I had begun with no prospects—
as the wiseacres said—and yet had pros-
pered ; so she imagined that the chances
were against her."

" Did she dwell much on this ?" asked
Uncle Joe with some anxiety.

" No, I laughed her out of it. She
was a happy girl at last, thank God ! and
so grateful and loving. Her last words to
me were—I shall never forget them—

' *You are so kind. You are all so kind to me. O Bell! dear sister, say that you will love me always. Promise you will love me always whatever may happen;'* " and Bell wept at the recollection.

" What could she have meant by whatever may happen ?"

" That fear of bad luck. Oh, uncle! how awfully it was realised. If I had only persuaded her not to go out, or had gone with her."

" You did all for the best, my dear," said Uncle Joe, patting her hand. " You have nothing to reproach yourself with. I see you are fretting at what your father said. He was not in a state to know what he was saying. No one could have foreseen what happened."

" I am so glad you don't blame me," looking up with a tearful smile.

" Blame you ! No one in his senses could blame you."

" Of course I believed Mason that she had come in."

" Your father has discharged him."

" Oh how unfair ! The poor man thought he had seen her."

" It was not on that account; he got talking in the village, and behaved very badly. He told about your opening Travers' letter, and showing it to your father through the window. That, more than anything, gave rise to——"

" Yes, I know; please don't say the words. They make my flesh creep," Bell interrupts with a shudder. " The ungrateful wretch ! Was there no one true to us but dear old Jess ?"

" Your father has no very warm friends

there, I'm afraid," said Uncle Joe, evading
the question.

" Horace says—don't be offended, Uncle
Joe, Horace loved dear Madge like a sister
—he says that if money be wanted to trace
the thing out, he——"

" Is a good fellow.  No, my love ; I've
got the purse of Fortunatus here," and the
confident old gentleman tapped his forehead.

That night he spent at the Virginia, and
gently pumps its parcel-gilt youth about
the Honourable Mrs. Bletchingly.  Some
of them are acquainted with that lady, and
call Uncle Joe " an old rascal " behind his
back.  He has her address in his pocket-
book, next to that of Mr. Charles Watson ;
so he does not care.  He also gains some
further information about the mare Penelope, and those who " peppered " her so

boldly when she was at the shortest
odds, and all the knowing ones put down
the Muscatel Stakes as a "moral" for
her.

# CHAPTER VIII.

### MISSING.

HE flood which roared down the valley of the Beck for the better part of a week, has long since subsided. Mr. Pryor kept his promise to Kate Vane, and sent a boy every morning up Highstone Hill to look out for the white sheet which was to serve as a signal of distress from the mill. No such sign was made, and when the waters had gone down sufficiently to enable him to ride thither on horseback, he found the house deserted. No Kate, no letter, no message, no trace of her. " I do believe the poor thing is not quite right here," said Mrs. Aymes, tapping her forehead when Pryor brought the news. " She'd never have flown out as she did against Master Fraser if she was in her senses."

" She showed sense enough about that trench," replies the agent.

" What business had she at the mill at all?" demands the housekeeper. "I wouldn't have sent a dog out on such a night. Why couldn't she have stopped here quietly until the morning; or, if she wouldn't be beholden to us, have gone to some of her uncle's friends in the town? She'd have made a fine fuss if any one had told her to walk all that way in such weather."

" Well, Mrs. Aymes," Pryor replies, " it

.is a very lucky thing for us that she *did* go back, and I shall take good care of the furniture and things she has left behind her. I dare say she will write to some of us when she has settled."

"Settled! She'll never settle," is Mrs. Aymes' verdict. "But oh, Mr. Pryor, what an awful thing it is about that poor dear young lady!"

"You may well say awful," says he with a shudder.

"And she to have been married in two days. It's enough to break his heart, poor boy. Where is he—Mr. Fraser, I mean?"

"At Laremouth, I suppose."

"Then he did leave by the mail train that night?"

"I suppose so."

"He's forgot all about me and how I nursed him," muses the old housekeeper, with that far-off look which sometimes comes into the eyes of the aged ; " but I wish I were with him. He hasn't got kith nor kin to comfort him, Mr. Pryor, and he loved her very dear. I could see it in his face. It lit up like an angel's when he talked about her. Do you think they'll find—the body ?"

" For my own part, I hope not. I'm the County Coroner, you know, and I've seen such things. I hope that the sea will not give up her dead."

" Lord, Mr. Pryor ! How can you be so wicked ! That's as much as wishing she may not have Christian burial."

" Why should she not have Christian burial in the sea ? I would as soon be buried in the sea as in a churchyard. I'd as soon be buried under a rose-bush in my own garden as in Westminster Abbey."

"Yes, I know," said Mrs. Aymes,. bridling up. "You're one of those who talk of putting decent people under the earth in baskets. Oh! I've heard of that stuff; and I say you ought to be ashamed of yourself, and it's not—not respectable."

"That," said Pryor dryly, "is the beginning and end of the argument against it. It is respectable to wear silk and broadcloth in life, and oak and walnut in death. When one has said that a thing 'isn't respectable,' there is an end of the question. Nevertheless, I adhere to what I said. I hope that the remains of poor Miss Marston will not be found."

"If she were my child, I would never believe that she was dead till I saw her body."

"When one falls over two hundred feet of cliff——" Pryor began; but he changed his mind, and finished the sentence with a shrug.

His prophecy to Kate Vane about fever coming after the flood was realised. Cellars could be pumped clear of water, but not of slime. The weather became intensely hot. A vast expanse of mud, enriched with decaying vegetable matter and dead animals, weltered in the sun around Beckhampton. There was typhus in the town, and a bad type of what was locally known as " the shakes " out of it. Pryor put Fraser Ellicott's name down for five hundred pounds at the head of the relief fund, and the rest did their duty as—well, as usual in these islands, thank God! Those who could pay money, paid; and those who could work, worked.

There was little time for thinking what was going on at Laremouth, or anywhere

else, when men, women, and children were
sickening and dying, and the strongest did
not know when his time might come.
Pryor wrote many times to his chief at
different addresses, to confirm what he had
done, and order what else he should do;
but no replies came.

"I suppose he has gone abroad again, to
get over his own trouble," he told his wife;
"but I think it's just a little selfish, don't
you?"

"He knows you will do everything that
is right," said that lady; and her lord, who
did flatter himself that his proceedings
could not be amended, was satisfied.

No news came out respecting Kate
Vane; but people had long ceased to think
about her.

With autumn the fever abated. Poor
farmers were repaid the value of the cattle

they had lost; and I am sorry to say there were more claims put in than car-casses found. I should not state this fact if it had not some bearing upon what is to follow. Pryor, who was chairman of the relief committee, made diligent search for, and careful count of, dead beasts; and no one was paid compensation who could not prove his loss by producing the carcass, or part of it. Still not a word from the squire.

Old Hazeltine's enemies, the Steam Mills (Limited), having gone into liquidation in the physical as well as legal sense of the word, a tenant appeared for their once suffering rival, which, thanks to Kate Vane, had so bravely stood the flood; and terms were made with the refractory Beck. Slices of land which had been filched from his bed, here and there, were restored to it, obstructions removed, and the channel deepened. As he had extra work forced upon him, it was only fair he should have extra elbow-room to do it.

Gentlemen came from London, and calculated his flow to a gallon, and his capacity to a foot. But, alas for the trout! The " guid man " who had promised to restore the fishing was "awa'," and strictly utilitarian principles prevailed. Many a pretty tinkling fall, under which those speckled epicures loved to select their repasts, was abolished. Many a once glittering shallow dug out.

Widow Banfield, warned by the total loss of her crop, allowed a safety culvert to be made through her meadow, and Dr. Byng did not rebuild his Fives Court.

Whilst removing the pile of bricks which were once its wall, the labourers found an

instrument facetiously called a "life pre-
server"—six inches of twisted whalebone
and a pound of lead—forming a weapon
with which a child could brain Hercules.
How got it there? It was apparently
quite new. Nobody admitted having lost
such a thing, and no one wanted it.

So by Christmas all traces of the flood
had disappeared, and precautions had
been taken against the recurrence of a
similar calamity. This Pryor felt bound
to do upon his own responsibility.

It was not a merry Christmas for Beckhampton. There were more black than
coloured dresses in church, and it was a
mockery to wish many of its denizens a
happy New Year. The Hall was shut up.
Still not a word from the Squire. His
agent has breathing-time now, and is
troubled. Rent-day is at hand, and there

is hardly a tenant who has not some excuse or demand arising out of the flood. He is sitting in his office nibbing a pen, and bewailing the selfishness of youthful proprietors, when to his intense astonishment, Mrs. Wybert is announced.

" You never were a friend of mine," she begins, without any sort of salutation ; "never pretended to be ; and therefore I have come to you for advice."

" Pray be seated, madam," he begins in his usual client's voice, advancing the usual client's chair.

" I would rather stand," she replies, folding her hands under her black shawl. " I have not much to say, and I want it said and over. How long does it take to go to Barbadoes ?"

" I am a lawyer and estate agent, Mrs. Wybert. I do not profess to answer such questions—that is to such as come to me and say, as a preliminary, I am not their friend and never pretended to be."

" I did not come to consult you as a lawyer. I thought that after having wasted the best years of my life in this place, I might find one man whom it has enriched, willing to help me by answering a simple question, without being paid for it."

" I did not ask you to pay me, madam; I simply——"

" Evaded my demand. Will you tell me how long it takes to go to Barbadoes ? you can if you will. If you will not, I shall know what to think."

" Oh, you can think what you please. Here is Whitaker's Almanack—a wonderfully comprehensive work. I think it gives a table of Foreign Mails, yes, here it is. The mails appear to take about two months to come and go."

" Consequently," said the widow quickly, " I should have heard from my son on or about the 28th August. More than four months have passed since then, and I have not received a line."

" That is probably because he has not written."

" My son would not fail to write to me."

" If he did write, the post-office authorities would not fail to deliver you his letter, madam."

" You insinuate that he neglects me ? his mother !"

" I never insinuate."

" Yes you do, sir; you say that if he had written, I should have his letter. I had previously told you that I had not re-

ceived a line. This is as much as to say
that he has neglected me. Please try to
forget that you are a lawyer, Mr. Pryor.
Forget, if you can, that I am what I
dare say.many people call a disagreeable
old woman. Forget what I said about
not being my friend — I meant that
to show that I only wanted the truth
from you—and tell me what does it
mean ?"

There are tears in her voice, but none in
her eyes. . A lawyer aged forty, who is not
a judge of character, has sadly misused his
opportunities. A lawyer who has used his
opportunities knows the bitterness of some
hearts—however well they may seek to
hide it—nearly as well as they do themselves. Mr. Pryor saw right through the
woman who had come to him because he
had never pretended to be her friend.

" I do not exactly understand why you should ask me such a question," he says. " It seems to me you can answer it best for yourself; but as you have put it, and in such a way; and as you are one of those people who deal in home truths—I should say he does not write either because he does not want to do so, or because——"

" He is dead ?"

" That is what I was going to say."

" If he be dead, I know who threatened his life," she replies fiercely.

" And will not forget it whenever it be convenient to remember the circumstance," said Pryor.

" Be sure of that ! Be quite sure of that, Mr. Pryor. I have heard words which haunt me day and night. At first I thought them an empty brag. Latterly they— Do you think that hate can kill

without hands ? If so—pshaw! you are a
lawyer. Tell me what has become of your
grand young patron whose lady-love committed suicide ?"

" She did not commit suicide."

" They say so."

" They ! Let me tell you, Mrs. Wybert
that such people as are called ' they ' in
cases like this, should be scourged at the
cart's tail," cried Pryor the man ; Pryor the
lawyer had disappeared.

" Oh, of course !" she sneers, " Miss
Marston was a clergyman's daughter. I
quite understand. And the man to whom
she was going to be married in two days
disappears. Quite correct, of course ! But
if some poor girl had taken strychnine in
such a case, we should have known what
to think. Pity for justice that the body
has not been found and an inquest held,

29—2

More pity, perhaps, for some, if it were found."

" One has to bear a good deal from your sex, Mrs. Wybert," said Pryor, " because they are women ; but when a woman says things which put her out of the pale of womankind, one sees only a thing which one cannot knock down because it is not a man ; or ignore because it is not an idiot, or kill because it is not a beast.  We can only avoid it, as I do, by leaving the room."  And (to use a new expression) he suited the action to the word.

I cannot give you a better insight into the character of the person whom he left standing there, than by telling you that she could not understand why he had thus abruptly left her, and that she went out of his office muttering something about his rudeness.

ᵕPryor went and kissed his girls, and
that did him some good. He also had a
fling at Fraser Ellicott which helped to
blow off his steam.

"His treatment of me is outrageous,"
he fumed. "He imposes upon me. He
has no right to throw all this responsibility
and worry upon me, and I'll let him know
it. If I don't hear from him by the end
of the month, I'll throw the whole thing
up. That will bring him."

"Why don't you apply to his bankers
in London?" suggests madame, who did
not approve the idea of throwing up.
"They must know where he is."

"As if I hadn't thought of that!" sneers
Pryor. "Why, that's the first thing I
did. He drew five hundred for his honey-
moon tour, and he had six thousand in
bank notes from his trustees. He won't

want money for some time to come.    If
he wanted anything he'd pretty soon let
me know," snapped his agent.

" Ah, poor fellow ! you mustn't be too
hard upon him," the lady pleads.    " Only
think what a dreadful shock."

" It seems odd," Pryor continues, some-
what pacified, " that he did not go to
Laremouth.    They have an abominable
story down there that he jilted the poor
girl, and she flung herself from the cliff in
consequence."

" You never told me that !"

" Why should I ?    I detest scandal, and
only mention it now because that old
harridan Wybert has got hold of it some-
how, and it will be all over the town
to-morrow.    You must contradict it, my
dear.    His last words to me when we left
the Rose and Crown that night were :

' Well, Pryor, I shall be a married man when next we meet. Sorry you can't come to the wedding, but don't forget to drink our healths.' That don't sound like jilting."

" Still, as you say, it is odd he did not go there afterwards, if only to hear all the details," replies Mrs. Pryor. " I should never have been satisfied until I had seen the place and searched everywhere myself. Why, they have never found the body yet! He seems to have taken everything for granted and gone abroad."

" You were making excuses for him just now."

" He is greatly to be pitied, Pryor, whatever has happened. Suppose he heard something bad in London about the girl, and broke off the marriage ? He is more to be pitied than ever then,

considering what has happened. Good
heavens, if it should turn out that he
acted hastily—he would be a murderer !"

" You are supposing that she committed
suicide ?"

" No. If she had gone out miserable
and reckless, and an accident happened—
it would be all the same."

" Pshaw ! she went out perfectly happy.
You read Mrs. De Gray's letter in answer
to mine inquiring about Ellicott. It was
a pure accident."

" Then why didn't he go and find out
all about it for himself ?"

" Nothing would please me better than
to know, my dear," says Pryor. " His
conduct is more than odd; but we must
not pretend to think so. I let the people
suppose I am in constant communication
with him. Keep your ears open, and if

you have any reason to believe that Mrs. Wybert has been spreading her scandal, let me know."

In the course of the next week Mrs. Pryor made several visits amongst the most voluble of her acquaintance, but heard nothing of the widow; except one fact which did not seem to be of much importance—namely, that the " Maid of the Mill" (as the local reporters had named Kate Vane) had turned up again, and was living with that lady.

Now the furniture abandoned by Kate had so embarrassed the new miller, that Pryor was obliged to have it carted away and stacked in an outhouse on his own premises. He didn't want to be bothered with it either; so as soon as he knew where to find her, he went and asked her what was to be done with it. This of course led to questioning. Why had she run away from the mill like that? Where had she been? and what had she been doing? Did she suppose she was going to get on with that old cat? (meaning Mrs. Wybert). She declined to satisfy Mr. Pryor's curiosity except with a playful self depreciation which disarmed it. *He* did not care to know. What could it possibly matter to *him?* Yes, the widow was hard and sometimes cross, but she thought they would manage to get on. Would he be so very good as to give her (Kate) Mr. Ellicott's address *as soon as he heard from him.*

This rather startled Mr. Pryor. How did this girl know that they were not in constant correspondence?

# CHAPTER IX.

## OUT OF MOURNING.

THE Honourable Mrs. Bletchingly is not in the great world, but is good enough to supply it with a great deal to talk about. Let me say at once that whatever she may have been, she is now a lawful wife, and an honest woman, learning the lesson that although there may be joy in heaven over one repentant sinner, the ninety and nine who think they sit in the seats of the just down here, take good care to discount it. Society (female) speaks of her as "that creature," and copies her dresses. Society (male) intrigues for an invitation to her small parties—"just to see the house, you know." And really the house is a sight to see. If the Forty Thieves had broken into the South Kensington Museum, and being pressed for time, had dumped the loot in a carver and gilder's shop, that establishment would present a striking resemblance to Mrs. Bletchingly's drawing-rooms. You cannot move three steps in any direction without seeing your face in a glass, and running the risk of upsetting something that is not to be matched.

About two years ago she said to herself, "I'll make the best of what I have, play the lady whilst it lasts, and marry the first rich fool who asks me." The Honourable Richard Bletchingly (second son of Lord St. Louis, and *par excellence the* fool of that noble family) exactly "fitted the bill," as they say on the other side of the Atlantic. She married him, and the fortune he had just inherited from a wealthy aunt, and makes him a much better wife than might be expected. She is handsome, clever, ambitious; knows how to dress herself, and when to hold her tongue. If she had only laid regular siege to the great world, and opened her approaches with patience and strategy, she might have scraped into its holy places; but she tried to take it by assault. The great world will not be taken by assault. Some of its outworks may be won by a well-sustained fire of champagne corks, and a picket or two driven in by a charge of the chariots of Longacre and the horses

of Yorkshire. But the grim citadel holds
out, and let us be thankful that it is so—
strong.

She has been happy enough in the outworks she has gained; for she lives in
hopes of obtaining the countersign which
will open the golden gates of that Heaven
whose mansions are mentioned in the
*Morning Post.* She has those wonderful
drawing-rooms, and such a boudoir! She
has horses, carriages, a box at the Royal
Italian Opera, a villa on the Thames,
diamonds and dresses galore! plenty of
money, good health, beauty, a semi-idiotic
husband who adores her, and latterly—a
ghost! For nearly three years she has
been afraid of ghosts, and for the last
three weeks she is haunted by one. No
spectre of dignified mien and solemn
aspect; but a wretched little apparition

with the eyes of a pig and the jaw of a
prize-fighter, with a husky voice and bandy
legs; a ghost that might have mounted
Death's pale horse at about seven stone
nine, and that carried an atmosphere, not
of brimstone, but second-hand gin and
field onions about him. He (for this
ghost is masculine) calls her " Sally," and
reminds her of a certain five hundred
pounds. If he would take five thousand,
and drink himself to death with it, she
would fall on her knees and thank Heaven
for its mercies—but he won't. He can
drink himself as far as he wants to go at
present upon small sums, and he is cunning,
is this ghost—he doesn't want much at a
time. He is afraid to have money about
him. He takes a malicious delight in
haunting the house that is a sight to see,
and the lady for whose acquaintance so

many of the parcel-gilt youth are sighing
in vain, is never denied to him. Wretched
Mrs. Bletchingly! If those who envy
her only knew what nights and days she
passes! If those who call her "that
creature," and rather disapprove of Providence for permitting her to enjoy such
splendour, only saw into her heart! How
they would rejoice, the dear good Christian souls! Does she deserve her fate?
Uncle Joe, who bit by bit has mastered
the details of her history, thinks not; but
then Uncle Joe is of the world, you know,
and a man. Men always find excuses for
"creatures." This one goes so far as to
assert that the lady is not a "creature"
at all, in the sense of the word used by the
just as they sit in judgment upon her in
their penny chairs. He admits that she
was brought up in a racing stable amongst

trainers and jockeys; that at one time she kept house for a triumvirate, composed of a suspended light weight, a betting list man, and a person with purple whiskers who called himself a major, and was a tout; that these worthies spent most of the little fortune which she inherited from her uncle; and that she ran away from them with what balance she could find, about the time of the Penelope affair.

Some of the great world lose all interest in her when they learn that she was only a fool in those younger days—made so by a man then in the zenith of his fame—a very Apollo as it seemed to her—the fashionable jockey of his day, whom sporting earls slapped on the back, and baronets begged to wear their colours. He was not known as Bill "the Roper" when he won her foolish young heart. Man-like, he trifled with her worship in his prosperity, and, woman-like, she stuck to him in his adversity—fed him, hid him, and lost her good name for his worthless sake. Uncle Joe stoutly denies that anything else was lost.

It would not have done the wretched haunted hunted woman of to-day any good to publish her now indignant, now abject —part piteous, part fierce protestations on this head. *Qui s'excuse, s'accuse*, is an excellent adage for the condemnation of " creatures." Throw plenty of dirt, and when they try to wipe some of it away, cry, " Oh, you defend yourself, do you ! Then you must be guilty."

There was no folly in what followed. It is not to be denied that the lady who is now the Honourable Mrs. Bletchingly went to Scarborough, and putting aside fifty pounds for board and lodging, sunk the rest of her capital in bait to be placed on a now very sharp hook. The fishing was not so great a crime as the catching. Had she landed a smaller fish, she might have carried him home in peace, perhaps ; but he was one of the takes of the season, and, as I have said before, she made too much of the capture.

All this comes out bit by bit. Uncle Joe has a difficult game to play. He cannot go to this lady and say : " Madam, you are haunted by a ghost—a bandy-legged ghost ; who smells of second-hand gin and field onions—permit me to lay him ?" He has first of all to ingratiate himself with her ; then to tell her all about the awful catastrophe at Laremouth, and give his reasons for wanting to find a certain William Sidebottom. He has to hint of

the folly of giving in to persecution, and
recount how the life of one man he had
known—an excellent honourable man—was
embittered because in a moment of weakness he had given a scoundrel five shillings
to hold his tongue ; and how another, by
taking heart (not exactly of grace) by in-
dicting the fellow, had hushed up what
was really a very shady transaction.   He,
I am writing of Uncle Joe, gets a footing
in the house which is a sight, and rigs a
delicately constructed, but powerful force-
pump amongst its crinkum-crankums.   Its
service-pipe goes down into the heart of its
mistress.   And oh ! the bitter waters that
flow.

It is good for her that they flow.   She
thinks Uncle Joe the kindest, wisest,
dearest (yes, she once called him a dear,
and kissed him in presence of her lord) of

men. And the great world is astonished at Sir Joseph Balderson. Sir Joseph is not to be entrapped into a defence of Mrs. Bletchingly. He is only curious to learn what there is against her, and is most provoking. He wants to know how people know this and that; and it is sad for man or woman, after having built up an imposing edifice of anger, hatred, and malice with second-hand materials, to be asked by this jaunty old Baronet where they got the stuff. He blinks not the truth. Her father was a gentleman, her mother a farmer's daughter; she was brought up very badly, and she fished with three costumes by Worth for a rich husband—what else? Somebody has told everybody a good deal else, but when Uncle Joe edges up his chair and blandly asks, "Please tell me all you know," nobody knows anything. Some who start like roaring lions about to devour this lady's character, are made to coo as softly as any sucking dove by one word — "Penelope." Uncle Joe *knows* about Penelope. So successful is our diplomatist that Lady St. Louis is induced to call upon the "creature" and make the best of a bad business.

It is only after this grand *coup* that Uncle Joe comes to his point, and asks that William Sidebottom, *alias* Bill "the Roper," should be given into his hand. Bill's hold over Sally Vane "grows out" (to use a famous phrase) of that five hundred pounds—the wages of his sin in the Penelope affair.

"She stole it," says Bill.

"No," pleads Uncle Joe, "she only re-paid herself what you had spent of her own money, and if you make any more fuss about this, the missing links of evidence against you will be supplied."

" You can't prosecute me twice for the same thing," says Bill, with his tongue in his cheek.

" Perhaps not," admits the other side ; "but how about the sovereign you embezzled at Ramsden Junction ?"

The discussion ends by Bill promising solemnly to take twenty pounds a month, and behave himself ; or a thousand down and go to America, where he is assured by Sir Joseph there are wide roping fields spoiling for want of him. It does not, however, suit Sir Joseph that he should seek those happy pastures just yet. He has yet to tell who it was that hired that horse on the night of the 28th July. Mr. Sidebottom does not know the gentleman's name, never saw him before ; but has seen him since. In London ? Yes, he is quite sure of that. The gentleman wore a pair of blue specs, but he knowed him, and should know him again. It is made worth Mr. Sidebottom's while to know him again, to follow him, and see where he lives, and to find out all about him.

It must not be supposed that because the result of these negotiations can be thus glibly stated, the task of their author was a short or easy one. He had many rebuffs, disappointments, and failures ; and autumn had come and passed into winter before they were—so far—completed. He never loses sight of his main point—to find the man who had ridden over from Ramsden Junction, and sent that letter to Madge—the man who (as he firmly believes, in spite of all that Mr. Marston can say to the contrary) had passed his study window on that wretched night. Mr. Marston is no longer Vicar of Laremouth. He has effected that exchange, and is now incumbent of St. Christopher's, a fashionable place of worship situated not far from where Mr. Henry Wybert used to live. This—he is good enough to inform all and singular—has cost him a considerable sacrifice in point of income, but it brings him near his dear daughter, Mrs. De Gray; and really after his sad bereavement at his former living, and his brother-in-law's inconsiderate behaviour there, any change is beneficial. He shakes his head when he mentions his sad bereavement, and speaks of it in that palate tone which I observe is used by most clergymen when upon serious topics ; but he has quite recovered his old sprightly manner, takes delight in the furnishing of his rooms, which become in their way as great a sight as those of Mrs. Bletchingly, and has plenty of ready money.

Nor is he hard upon Uncle Joe for that "inconsiderate conduct." He informs Bell that her uncle would have made an excellent detective, but is too visionary—far too visionary.

"Your father, my dear," says Sir Joseph, *contra*, "is a very talented man, but he has not one grain of common sense!"

Bill "the Roper" does not lose sight of his work, nor does Uncle Joe lose sight of him. He has not again seen the man with the blue spectacles; and reports early in January, with much alarm, that he finds he is himself watched.

"You ain't gone back upon me, governor," he whines, "have yer? cause there's a party arter me looking up that same party as you're a looking arter."

" Some one else on the same track ! what can that mean ?" muses Sir Joseph. " Had the police whom he slighted and ignored hit upon the very suspicion that had struck him ?  Well, no matter if they had."

In the course of a few days Mr. Marston's brother, the earl, writes from Paris to say that being known as an amateur of pearls, a clasp composed of those gems, and which bears a striking resemblance to that belonging to the necklet he had sent as a wedding present to Madge, has been offered to him for purchase !  Surely they had not sold his gift ?

" Why, good heavens !" cried Bell, " our poor lost darling wore it that night."

Mr. Marston writes back that there must be some mistake, and receives a stiff reply. There was no mistake. It was a shame and a folly to break up such a necklet, for all the pearls matched. This correspondence is addressed to Bell, as the earl does not know her father's present address. Uncle Joe is present when it arrives; and "Now!" he cries triumphantly, " what does that prove ?"

" That my brother is a very obstinate person," replies the Rev. Mr. Marston, " and not the only one in the family."

" Or out of it," retorts Uncle Joe. " Let me see now. There is an obstinate ostler, late of Ramsden Junction; an obstinate boy at Laremouth ; an obstinate butler out of place named Mason; an obstinate clerk and sexton named Probert; an obstinate person, name unknown, who is looking after the obstinate ex-ostler ; and lastly, an obstinate peer of the realm who resides in Paris and is a judge of pearls. There is also an obstinate gate which was opened by the owls and would not shut itself, and an obstinate horse."

" Do you think it is quite in good taste to make a jest of this ?" asks Mr. Marston, biting his lip.

" A jest of it ?" cries Sir Joseph. " By heavens ! it is becoming more and more serious every day. You are the only one who tries to jibe away the facts."

" I will not get angry with you, brother Joseph," bleats Mr. Marston, " because I am certain that you mean well. I have already shown you what little importance is to be attached to things you call *facts*. This you call jibing at them ! Well, let it pass, and now about the pearl clasp.

Grant that my brother is correct, and it did belong to that necklet—what then? It shows that my poor child's body has been found at sea—most probably by some French fishermen; and—oh! it is very painful, I cannot go on. I do *so* wish you would take a rational view of things. You want to make out that some man came to Ramsden Junction and hired a horse, and rode to Laremouth with a letter to entice my child out in order to rob her of a jewel which he could not know that she even possessed—much less wore."

"I do not contend that he came on purpose to rob her."

"Then what did he come for?"

"That is to be found out. I shall go to Paris and see if I cannot trace that clasp."

"I hope you will not," moans the ex-

Vicar. " Dear ! dear ! It seems so sad that my poor child is not allowed to rest in peace. What good *can* you do ? Gain some harrowing details as to how her poor corpse was found. Brother Joseph, if you have any regard for my feelings—and surely they are to be consulted ?—you will let this matter drop."

Uncle Joe is sadly perplexed. He does not want to let it drop. He cannot well refuse such an appeal. He stands with his chin in his hand pondering how he can parry it ; when a servant enters, and says that there is a man downstairs who wants to see Sir Joseph *very particular.* Sir Joseph, glad to escape without committing himself, goes down and finds Mr. William Sidebottom in the hall.

" I've seen him, sir," whispers that worthy, " and found out where he lives."

" The man who hired the horse at Ramsden Junction ?"

" I'll swear to him, and I can take you to the house this directly minute if you like."

" No, that would not do. What is his name ?"

" Mr. Wybert."

" Impossible !" cries Uncle Joe, aghast.

" Fact," replies Bill " the Roper," twisting the straw in his mouth.

" Did he recognise you ?"

" Yes, he did ; and it's my opinion that if you don't make sure of him pretty sharp he'll give you the slip again—him and the lady too."

" What lady, man ?"

" Well, his wife I suppose ; leastwise they call her Mrs. Wybert."

" Come in here," says the Baronet,

opening the study door, "I must hear more of this."

Bill follows, after much punishment of the mat; Uncle Joe takes a seat by the fire, and assumes the mien of an examining magistrate. Bill advances—as he is motioned—to the hearthrug, and looks around him. There are two portraits—photographs in shrine frames on the mantelpiece. The gilded doors which guard one of them are generally closed before the sweet sad face; but to-day, for some reason, they are wide open. As soon as Bill's eye falls on that photograph, he exclaims:

"Good Lord! why, that's her!"

"That is Miss Marston who fell over the cliff at Laremouth," says Uncle Joe.

"That's Mrs. Wybert as lives in Dale Street, Camberwell," cries Bill "the Roper."

\*     \*     \*     \*     \*

" You can take off your mourning," Uncle Joe tells them when he goes upstairs again half an hour afterwards. " We have all been deceived—cruelly. Madge did not fall over the cliff that night. She eloped with Henry Wybert !"

# CHAPTER X.

### "SHE MIGHT BE STARVING."

IT would not edify the reader for me to set up before him the machinery of threats and pit-falls, promises of indemnity and reward, by means of which Uncle Joe got out of Mr. William Sidebottom all of his share in the events of the night of the 28th June. Hitherto he had only been questioned about the gentleman who hired the horse. Let us be content with results. Mr. Sidebottom had been " given the sack " that afternoon, and was loafing about the station, not knowing where to go or what to do, when the 8.35 train came in, and with it a traveller with a long coat over his arm, and his head tied up in a scarf, as though he "had the face-ache bad." *He* also did not seem to know what to do or where to go, but eventually sidled up to the ex-ostler, and asked him if he could get him a horse without telling any one. Bill was not able to procure one otherwise. He knew where the stable key hung, watched his opportunity, and before long produced a steed which had been eating his " 'ed off for the last three weeks, and wanted exer-cise." Thus Bill was pleased to put it ; no other consideration than the good of the "'oss" moved him to bring it out that night. He was to meet the hirer again at

ten o'clock, and take it back to its stall.
Ten o'clock came, and eleven, but no
traveller, and Bill began to make sure that
he had been done, when up the gentleman
came, and not alone.   The long coat was
now worn by his companion.   The hood
covered that person's head, and the skirts
fell round that person's feet, and the gentleman called that person " George ;" but
Bill was not going to be " took in by any
such little game as that."   The person was
a lady, and she was a-crying pretty nigh
all the time, and he a-nudging of her and
whispering to keep up, and be brave " like
a darlin'—that's what he sed."   When the
mail was about due, they—"lesswise the
gentleman "—gave him (Bill) the money
to buy two first-class tickets for London,
and as they got into the train he had a
good sight of the lady's face, and he would

" lay fifty thou. to a brass farden that she was that lady," pointing to the photograph on the mantel. Why did he not speak? Had he not heard or read · of the awful catastrophe at Laremouth? Yes, he had; but how did he know the gentleman had been to Laremouth? "The lady as fell from the clift " was a clergyman's daughter —how could he think that a clergyman's daughter would be up to such capers as that?

He was walking along the Westminster Bridge Road with a pal of his, when he saw the gentleman again, and knew him in spite of his blue specs.

"When you give me the office, governor," he added, " I laid for him, and got my pal to help. He come out of a newspaper shop, and we found that he was mortal fond of reading newspapers—went there two or three times a week to buy all sorts. Well, we waited on him, and tracked him home at last; but, Lord! he was skeery— gave us the slip a score of times; so I hope I've earned the reward."

" If you are telling the truth, you have," said Uncle Joe.  " How did you discover his name ?"

" From the landlady where they lodge."

" Now tell me about the other party— as you call him—who has been inquiring after them."

" If you'd believe me, sir," replies Bill, lowering his voice, " I believe he's a detective ?"

" Why so ?"

" Because he was so civil.  'Mr. Sidebottom,' says he, taking off his hat. 'You've the advantage of me,' ses I. 'Late stud-groom at the Ramsden Arms,' ses he, not minding a bit what I sed. 'Have you seen that party as hired a 'oss of you on the 28th June, lately?' he ses. 'I don't let 'osses,' ses I. 'It would be rather a good thing for you,' he ses, 'if you did,' he ses, 'and could say who you let it to.' I've spotted him many a time follering me, and hanging about that newspaper shop."

"He is on a fool's errand," says Uncle Joe bitterly, "and is not the only fool that Mr. Wybert has made. Now be careful. Do you persist in saying that the lady who was with him that night is the original of this picture?"

"Yes, I do."

"It was night when you saw her, and she had the hood of that coat over her head."

"Guv'ner, I saw her this morning in

broad daylight, and she had nothink over her 'ed," Bill replies, with some solemnity; " but if so be as you don't want it to be her, why I don't mind swearing——"

" You scoundrel ! Do you think I want you to tell lies ? The truth is bad enough, God knows !" he adds to himself. " Stay here ; I may want you again."

Then he went up, and told them they might take off their mourning.

Bell was the first to make an articulate reply, or to ask a rational question. A crowd of remembrances chased each other through her brain; Madge's anxiety to make peace with Wybert ; her fears of not being "safe" with Fraser Ellicott ; her fancy that she would bring him bad luck ; her questions as to how men bear disappointment in love ; her strange words at parting on that awful night—"*You will love me always, whatever may happen?*"—all came back with a vividness they had never had before. She also remembered her own sisterly advice not to marry one man if a latent spark of affection for another lingered in her bosom. And this was the result!

Madge had worried herself into the belief that she loved Henry Wybert. He had taken advantage of her morbid musings, and got her to elope with him. She was not dead, but had buried all that was good, and true, and lovable of her under mountains of cruelty and falsehood.

"Oh! how could she treat us thus—we who loved her so!" is all that poor Bell can moan.

Her father's conduct is strange. He is not surprised to hear that his daughter is alive—only frightened. He is not angry at learning her falsehood—only furious with "that ruffian," as he calls Mr. William Sidebottom. I have known other people who are moved, not at a shameful discovery, but against the discoverer.

"I have been so mistaken," says Uncle Joe, with tears in his honest old eyes, "that I hardly like to say what I think now."

"Oh! do go on!" pleads Bell. "What can it mean?"

"She must have had a lurking tenderness for that fellow, which poor Fraser could not dispel. Do you know that she met him whilst she was staying here?"

"No! Did she?"

"She said so. She was very hurt at what I told her about his having failed, and spoke to him about it. God knows how often they met afterwards!"

"If she had only been honest with Fraser, and broken it off!"

"She had not the moral courage; and he, that Wybert, like a villain, took advantage of her when she was most nervous and unstrung."

"They are married, Uncle Joe?"

"Of course. Trust Madge, with all her faults, for that; and doubly trust him."

"You see, papa," Bell observes, after a long pause, "Mason was right; Mr. Wybert passed your window that night."

"He did *not*," says Mr. Marston doggedly.

"Then it must have been Madge herself."

"What is the use of speculating in this way?" he cries, starting to his feet, and

pacing the room with pale lips and falter-
ing breath. "See where your speculations
have led you! You made her fall over
the cliff; you made her throw herself
over the cliff; you made a robber throw
her over. You were wrong every way.
In God's name, why go on guessing? Is
not the fact that she has disgraced us all
enough for you?"

"It is enough for me," Uncle Joe replies. "I have done with her. I was
never so deceived in my life. If I had
been asked to pick out a girl who could be
relied upon, under all circumstances, to be
honest and true, I would have pointed to
Madge. I was proud of her, and—and
d——e, I loved her. If she had been my
own child, I could not have loved her
more than I did."

"My dear brother," says Mr. Marston,

taking his hand and whimpering, " I honour your sentiments, and deeply deplore the sad ingratitude with which they have been requited; but you are right—you are right and wise, as you generally are. How seldom it is that we find a warm heart under a discreet head ! Painful as it may be, your verdict is a just one—the only one at which we can arrive with any self-respect. My unhappy daughter has taken her own headstrong course, and must follow it to the end. As you very properly say, we have done with her. I will never see her again. I must beg, Bell, that you will not again mention her name. She is dead to us. I would rather have heard the sods fall on her coffin than the words my kind brother has spoken to-day." And he wept.

He left them soon afterwards; he was

so shocked, so unmanned. He must go home, and try to compose himself.

Bell took it differently.

"Please don't go, uncle," she pleaded, "till Horace comes. I—I am afraid to be alone with my thoughts. I want to know more, to think more with some one. I know it *is*. I want to be sure *how* it is. I want to find some excuse for Madge, Uncle Joe ; there *must* be some excuse for her."

"I have been puzzling over Fraser's letter," said he.

"What letter ?"

"Why, that which came the day after —you know."

"Ah ! How stupid of me to forget that. Is it possible that he was not free to marry her, and Mr. Wybert found it out ?"

" Just the idea that was forming itself in my mind."

" And yet he would hardly have written that the marriage should only be postponed."

" His letter is altogether incoherent."

" He says in it that he could explain."

" I will do him the justice to admit that I do not believe he knew of any obstacle when he proposed for your sister. I suspect it was the fruit of some dragon's tooth he had sown without knowing it. Young men who travel much sometimes get into scrapes which don't show at first. Suppose, for example, he had got entrapped into what is called a marriage in Scotland ?"

" He could not explain that away."

" No ; but he could show that he had been a fool, and not a scoundrel."

"That is true. The discovery, or even the plot, might have been Wybert's work."

"The discovery perhaps."

"Why not the plot? He might have put the—the creature—up to claim him."

"He might," mused Uncle Joe.

"And making poor Madge believe that he was knowingly false, have turned her against him, and led her to revenge herself by eloping."

"Possibly. But why elope for revenge? She might, as you said just now, have broken off her engagement openly and honestly."

"The poor child was angry."

"Anger with Fraser could not justify her for such cruelty to us," said the Baronet bitterly.

"Oh! it was cruel—so cruel! How she must have suffered!"

" That's a woman all over," growls Uncle
Joe.    " If people hit you, you always pity
their poor knuckles."

This brought the conversation to an end
for a good half-hour, and the day closed in
silence.

" Where did that man say they were
living, Uncle Joe?" Bell asked, when the
gas was lit.

" At a lodging-house in Dale Terrace,
Camberwell."

" Are they poor ?"

" Who knows ? who cares ?   Serve them
right if they are."

" Oh, Uncle Joe !"

" I've no pity for such people."

" But, Uncle Joe, wouldn't it be only
fair to hear what she has to say, before we
condemn her ?"

" I see what you are driving at.   You

want to go and see her, and kiss and cry, and make it all up. I know you."

"And I know you. You'll come with me, dear Uncle Joe."

" Never."

"We can go to-night. She might be starving, for he has not a shilling."

"We can send her some money if you like."

" Better take it, and so be sure if it be wanted."

"There's no doubt of that."

" Fancy poor little Madge hungry and cold ; and perhaps ill-used !"

" Bell, you're a fool !"

" Uncle, you are crying !"

" I've got a confounded cold in my head," snorts the ex-diplomatist, sounding an alarm in his pocket-handkerchief.

"Stay and dine," says discreet Mrs. De

Gray, "and we will talk it over with Horace."

Now, this same Horace is a man who would write a cheque for a hundred guineas, and take it to Beelzebub himself, if told that he was in trouble. Give this man an estuary to bridge, or a mountain to abolish, and he will take in the idea as a bird drinks water—tell you to a man, a ton of iron, and a shilling, what he wants for the work; and to a day when he will have it done, bar strikes; but tell him a story against some one he likes, and a more obstinate, dunder-pated, and perverse person does not exist. He breaks four of Bell's pet fern-engraved glasses, when it comes out that Madge is not dead. He snorts defiance and incredulity when Mr. William Sidebottom's story is repeated. When Uncle Joe takes him in hand, and deliberately unrolls the chain of evidence which is to bear out that gentleman's statement, he gets terribly perplexed. How could Wybert have got hold of Fraser's letter, and what the deuce would Madge want eloping with that boy? When it is impressed upon him that there are two letters (one of which did not arrive until next morning) and that Madge had left with the boy's employer, he gets a little clearer, and asks this rather pertinent question. If Madge and Wybert met at the thinking-place, and Bell's nubia were dropped or thrown from the cliff there, what the —— (let us say *diable,* as naughty things may be said in French) did either of them want humbugging about in the Vicarage garden afterwards? This is not explained, and the man of the house snorts more defiance and incredulity. Told that he can settle the whole question in a hansom for half-a-crown, he is for dashing off at once, but is checked by Uncle Joe.

"We have no right to interfere without consulting Mr. Marston," he urges. "Let us go round to him, and see what he will do."

"And if he won't do anything?" says Bell in a piteous tone.

"Then, my dear," replies her uncle, "we can—yes, we can do——"

"Without him," interrupts Horace De Gray decisively.

So they drive round to Mr. Marston's chambers, and he is not at home. They learn with surprise that he has not been at home since the morning. Where then has he gone to "compose" himself? To his club? Not a very good place in which to seek solitude and composure; nevertheless they call at his club. He has not been there all day! Well, they have done their best to find him. By this time they are all wound up into a high state of anxiety and excitement. They are out to know the worst of it, and no one wants to turn back now. On to Camberwell is the cry; and on they go.

It is eight o'clock, and a Saturday night. The streets are ablaze with portable gas, and resonant with cries for the sale of all sorts of commodities, from envelopes to onions. They turn from the busy thorough-fare into streets more and more low-spirited until they come to a railway embankment, under the shadow of which some enter-prising builder has stuck a row of stucco-fronted, bay-windowed, leaky, ten-roomed houses, with the view, apparently, that no one should ever be able to find them; or,

having found, should fly the dismal pros-
pect. If a bad Fairy were to bestow
some evil chance upon a Princess in these
days, there would be no necessity to build
her a tower of brass for her protection
against the outer world. Her parents and
guardians would only have to rent a house
in Dale Terrace and she would be lost to
human ken. It led nowhere. It was at
the end of a street which appeared to be
the end of all things, except the railway
embankment. The cabman knew it not.
The policeman on the beat could not say he
had heard of it. They did find it though,
and in this wise. As they inquired, a crowd
of children and idlers surrounded the cab.

"Dale Terrace," said a gentleman who
was passing, and asked what was the matter. "Oh yes, I can direct you. Take
the first——"

But he got no further. Bell, who was nearest the door, and the light, cried :

" Good gracious, papa !"

The Reverend Mr. Marston wished that the ground would open and swallow him.

END OF VOL. II.

BILLING AND SONS, PRINTERS, GUILDFORD, SURREY.

*S. & H.*

www.ingramcontent.com/pod-product-compliance
Lightning Source LLC
Chambersburg PA
CBHW020119030726
47498CB00006B/2186